A TREASURY OF FAIRY TALES

A TREASURY OF FAIRY TALES

Illustrated by Annie-Claude Martin

TRANSEDITION BOOKS

French-language edition
© 1988 by Éditions Nathan, Paris, France
        Le grand livre des contes
© 1990 by Éditions Nathan, Paris, France
        Grand contes merveilleux
© 1987 by Éditions Nathan, Paris, France
        Grand contes célèbres
Published by Éditions Nathan, Paris

Illustrations by Annie-Claude Martin

American-language edition
© 1994 Transedition Books,
a division of Andromeda Oxford Limited.

This edition published in 1994 in the United States
by Transedition Books, a division of
Andromeda Oxford Limited,
11–15 The Vineyard, Abingdon,
Oxfordshire OX14 3PX, England

Printed in 1994 in Spain

ISBN 1 89825 026 X

CONTENTS

(All tales have been retold)

Little Red Riding Hood

Once upon a time there was a little village girl, the prettiest you have ever seen. Her mother loved her dearly, as did her grandmother. She had made her a little red hood which suited her so well that everyone called her Little Red Riding Hood.

One day her mother said to her, "Your grandmother is not very well. Go and see how she is – you can take her some cookies and this homemade jar of jelly."

Little Red Riding Hood left right away to visit her grandmother who lived in another village. As

she was walking through the forest she met a wolf. He would have liked to gobble her up on the spot, but he did not dare to because there were some woodcutters nearby in the forest. He pretended to be very kind and asked her where she was going.

The poor girl did not know that it was dangerous to talk to a wolf and she said to him, "I am going to see my grandmother, to take her some cookies and a jar of jelly my mother made for her."

"Does she live very far away?" asked the wolf.

"Oh yes," replied Little Red Riding Hood, "her house is beyond the mill, by the first house in the village."

"Well," said the wolf. "I would like to see her too. I will take this road here, and you take the other road, and we will see who arrives first."

The wolf set off on the shortest path, running as fast as he could, while the little girl went by the other, longer path, amusing herself by gathering nuts, running after butterflies and picking small bunches of flowers.

It did not take the wolf very long to reach the grandmother's house.

He reached up and knocked at the door.

Tap, tap.

"Who is it?" came a voice from inside.

"It is your granddaughter, Little Red Riding Hood," said the wolf, disguising his voice. "I have brought you some cookies and a jar of jelly my mother has made for you."

The good grandmother, who was in bed, called out, "Lift up the latch and come in."

The wolf lifted the latch and the door opened.

At once he leapt on to the bed and ate up the poor woman in less than a second! Then he closed the door and laid down in the grandmother's bed to wait for Little Red Riding Hood

A few moments later she knocked at the door.

Tap, tap.

"Who is it?" came the gruff wolf's voice.

When she heard this Little Red Riding Hood was a little scared at first, but remembering her grandmother was ill she answered, "It is your granddaughter, Little Red Riding Hood. I've brought you some cookies and a jar of jelly my mother has made for you."

The wolf softened his voice a little and called out, "Lift up the latch and come in."

Little Red Riding Hood lifted the latch and the door opened.

The wolf hid under the bed covers and said, "Put the cookies and the jar of jelly on the table, and come sit on the bed beside me."

Little Red Riding Hood climbed on to the bed and stared at her grandmother.

"Grandma, what big arms you have!" she cried.

"All the better to hug you with," the wolf replied.

"And Grandma, what big ears you have!"

"All the better to hear you with."

"Grandma, what big eyes you have!"

"All the better to see you with, my child."

"Grandma, what big teeth you have!" cried Little Red Riding Hood.

"All the better to eat you with!" barked the wolf and, throwing back the covers, he leapt out of bed.

Just as he was about to eat up the little girl, the woodcutter who had been in the forest burst into the cottage. With one blow of his axe he cut off the wolf's head and nobody was ever troubled by that wicked creature again.

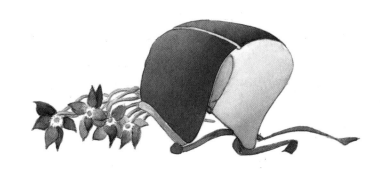

Snow White
and Rose Red

Once upon a time a poor widow lived in a hut in a lonely place. In front of the hut was a garden in which grew two rose bushes, one with white roses and the other with red. The widow had two daughters just like the two rose bushes and they were called Snow White and Rose Red.

The girls were very kind and obedient, and everyone who met them thought they must be the nicest girls in the world. Rose Red loved to run through fields and the meadows, picking flowers and chasing butterflies, but Snow White preferred

to stay with her mother at home, helping her with the housework and reading to her when the work was finished.

The sisters loved each other so much that they always held hands when they left the house and vowed that they would never be parted as long as they lived.

They often walked in the forest picking fruit. The animals never hurt them – they trusted the girls so much that they would walk up to them. The hare ate clover from their hands; the deer grazed beside them; the elk danced around them and the birds perched on the branches above them, singing beautiful songs to the girls.

If they stayed late in the forest and it became too dark to find their way home, they would sleep side by side in the moss until the next morning. Their mother knew they were safe there and never worried about them.

One time when they had spent the night in the forest they awoke at dawn and saw a beautiful child in a bright white dress standing in front of them. She looked at them kindly but said nothing, and then she disappeared into the forest.

When the girls looked around they discovered

that they had been sleeping at the very edge of a cliff. They would certainly have fallen in if they had walked just two more steps in the darkness. Their mother was sure that the child must have been the guardian angel of good children.

Snow White and Rose Red kept their mother's hut so clean that it was always a pleasure to look at.

In the summer, Rose Red did the housework every morning before her mother awoke. Then she would place a bunch of flowers beside her bed in

which there was one rose from each bush.

In the winter, Snow White lit the fire and hung the kettle on the pot hanger. This big copper kettle glittered like gold in the firelight because she had polished it so well.

In the evening when the snow fell their mother would say, "Snow White, bolt the door please."

Then they sat by the fireside. Their mother put her glasses on and read to the children from a big book, and the two young girls spun wool while they listened.

Their pet lamb slept at their feet and behind them, on its perch, slept a white turtle dove, with its head tucked under its wing.

One night when they were all sitting peacefully together there was a knock at the door.

"Rose Red, open the door quickly," said her mother. "It might be a traveller who is looking for shelter."

Rose Red pulled back the bolt, expecting to see a poor man but, to her great surprise, a bear put his big head through the doorway. Rose Red screamed and jumped back. The lamb began bleating, the turtle dove started fluttering about and Snow White hid behind her mother's chair.

Then the bear began to speak: "Don't be afraid, I won't do you any harm. I am half frozen and I only want to warm myself a little."

"Poor bear," said the mother. "Lie down near the fire, but be careful not to burn your fur."

Then she said, "Snow White, Rose Red, come here my children. The bear will not hurt you."

So they both came closer. Little by little the lamb and the turtle dove also approached and were not afraid of him any longer.

Then the bear said, "My children, would you mind brushing the snow off my fur?"

So they went to get the broom and cleaned the bear's fur. Then he stretched out by the fire, rumbling gently with comfort and pleasure.

The girls soon felt so sure of the bear that they began to tease their large guest. They pulled his fur with their hands, put their little feet on his back, rolled him from side to side, patted him with a stick and burst out laughing when he growled.

The bear let them play, but if it became too rough he said, "Children, leave me in peace:
> Snow White, Rose Red!
> Don't kill your sweetheart!"

When it was bedtime and the girls were asleep, their mother said to the bear, "You stay the night there, near the fire, and God will watch over you."

The next morning the two girls let the bear go when he asked and he went back into the forest, shuffling through the snow.

From then on he came back every evening at the same time to lie near the fire, and he let the girls play with him. They were so used to him by now that they did not bolt the door any more until after their friend came in.

When spring arrived and everything outside was green again, the bear said to Snow White one morning, "Now I have to leave you. You will not see me in the summer."

"Where are you going, dear bear?" asked Snow White.

"I have to go into the forest to protect all my treasures from the bad gnomes," he replied. "In the winter, when the land is completely frozen, the treasure is safe for they have to stay under the ground. Now the sun has warmed the ground they can make holes and get out. Everything they lay their hands on is taken back to their caves and never seen again."

Snow White opened the door for him, but she was very sad because he had to leave.

However, as the bear left, a little piece of his fur stuck in the latch. It seemed to Snow White that she saw gold glittering through the fur, but she was not absolutely sure.

The bear left quickly and soon he had disappeared behind the trees.

Some time later, the mother sent her children into the woods to gather twigs. On their way they found a huge tree lying on the ground, and around the trunk they saw something jumping about between the leaves, but they could not make out what it was.

When they came closer they saw it was a gnome. He had an old wrinkled face and a long white beard.

The end of his beard was caught in a crack of the tree and the little man was leaping from one side to the other like a chained dog, not knowing how to get out of this tangle.

He stared at the two young girls with his flaming eyes and cried, "What are you standing there for? Can't you come and help me?"

"Little man, what are you doing there?" asked Rose Red.

"You stupid, nosy goose," answered the gnome. "I wanted to chop down this tree to get some small logs for the kitchen. The big logs burn our little plates that we use to eat from, since we are not as greedy as you. I drove the wedge in with my axe, but the wedge was too shiny. It flew straight out and the crack closed so quickly that I had no time to pull out my beautiful white beard. Now I am stuck. Don't laugh at me, you naughty girls! Oh, you are very unkind!"

The children tried with all their might to pull the beard out of the tree, but it was impossible. It was completely stuck.

"I will go and find someone else to help us," said Rose Red.

"You stupid lamb!" grumbled the gnome. "What good would that do? There are already two of you here, and that is far too many! Can't you think of anything better?"

"Be patient," exclaimed Rose Red. "We will find a solution."

She took a pair of scissors from her pocket and cut the beard where it was caught. As soon as the

gnome was free he snatched up a bag filled with gold that was hidden between the roots of the tree.

He hugged it tightly and moaned, "Oh, what horrible scissors that dare to cut the end off my fine beard! I hope the devil will get you, you wicked girls!"

Then he swung the bag on his back and was off, without even thanking the children.

Another day, later in the summer, Snow White and Rose Red decided to go fishing.

When they arrived at the bank of the stream they saw what they thought was a grasshopper jumping at the side of the water.

They ran towards it and recognized the gnome.

"What are you doing?" asked Rose Red. "Do you want to jump into the water?"

"I am not stupid," answered the gnome. "Can't you see that fish trying to drag me into the water? Oh, it is an enchanted fish and I cannot break free of it!"

The little man told the girls that he had sat down with a rod and line, but a breeze had blown up and entangled the line in his beard, just when a big fish was biting it.

He wasn't able to pull it back since the fish was much stronger. The gnome tried to grab the blades of grass and rushes, but all in vain, and now he was in danger of being pulled into the water.

The two girls arrived just in time. They pulled at the line and tried to release the beard, but they had no more luck than the gnome – the beard and cord were quite entangled in each other.

At last the only thing they could think of to do was take the scissors and cut the beard, which made it much shorter!

When the gnome saw this he started to cry, "Do you have to be so stupid? Wasn't it enough to cut the end off my beard? Now you have taken the best part away from me and I am too embarrassed to go back to my friends. I hope you will get the punishment you deserve!"

Then the ungrateful gnome picked up a bag filled with pearls that was hidden in the reeds and, without saying another word, he disappeared behind a stone.

A few days later their mother sent the two young girls into town to buy some thread, needles, braid and ribbon. The path led across a field scattered with big rocks.

On their way they saw an eagle hovering overhead. Suddenly, as they watched, it swooped down behind a rock. Just as they were wondering what the big bird had spotted there they heard a loud and piercing shriek.

The girls ran towards the noise and saw that the eagle had grabbed their old friend the gnome and was trying to fly away with him.

The children quickly caught hold of the gnome's jacket and held on tight. The eagle flapped, the

31

gnome howled, and the children struggled and pulled. Eventually the effort became too much for the eagle, who had to give up and let go of its prey.

When the gnome had recovered from the shock he screamed with all his might, "Couldn't you have handled me a little more carefully? You have pulled so hard on my little jacket that it is torn to shreds, you horrible, clumsy girls!"

Then he picked up a bag filled with precious stones and slipped under the rock into his cave.

The young girls were used to his ungratefulness by now. They carried on towards the town to do their shopping, thinking no more about the horrid little man.

However, on their way back across the fields they again met the gnome. He was gloating over his hoard of precious stones and had not expected anyone to pass by at that time of the evening. The sunset made the stones sparkle and the sight was so beautiful that the girls stopped to look.

"What are you staring at with your monkey faces?" snapped the gnome when he saw them.

His pale face became as red as fire and he began to shout more insults at them in the hope that they

would decide to go away.

All of a sudden there was a terrible roar and a black bear came running from the woods.

The terrified gnome tried to hide, but the bear was too fast for him and quickly caught him with his huge paws. Then he started squealing and howling.

"Dear Mister Bear, spare me. I will give you all my treasures – look at the beautiful stones I have here. Don't kill me. What would you do with such a poor little man like me? You wouldn't even feel me between your teeth. Why don't you take those two wretched girls instead? They would make a delicious snack for you – they are as plump as a pair of geese. For goodness sake, eat them instead of me!"

The bear did not take any notice of what the gnome said and gave him one kick, which killed him instantly.

Then the bear called out to the two frightened girls, who were running away as fast as they could.

"Snow White, Rose Red, don't be afraid. Wait for me, I will go with you."

Suddenly the girls recognized his voice and

stopped running in delight. But when the creature
came closer to them his bearskin suddenly fell off,
and in front of them instead stood a young man,
dressed all in gold.

"I am a prince," he said. "I was bewitched by
that evil gnome, who stole all my treasures. He
made me run through the woods in the form of a
wild bear and said I would not be free of the spell
until his death. Now he has received the punishment he deserved."

Now, you might think that was the end of the story, but it wasn't quite. A few years later Snow White married the prince, and Rose Red married his brother.

The old mother lived with her children in peace and happiness ever after. She brought the rose bushes to the palace and planted them under the window, and every year they still bloomed with the most beautiful white and red roses in the world.

Hansel and Gretel

At the edge of a vast forest lived a poor woodcutter with his wife and their two children. The little boy was called Hansel and the little girl Gretel, and the family were so poor they had hardly anything to eat. Even worse, a great famine was threatening the land and the woodcutter was finding it very hard to make a living.

One evening, when the children had gone to bed, the man sighed and said to his wife, "What is to become of us? How are we going to feed our children when we don't even have anything for ourselves?"

"Well, I have a good idea," answered his wife. "Tomorrow, early in the morning, we will take the children to the thickest and darkest place in the forest. We will light a fire for them and give them each a piece of bread, then we will go to our work and leave them there. They will not be able to find the way back home and we will be rid of them."

"No," said the man. "I don't want to do that. How could I abandon my children in the forest? The wild animals will eat them."

"Oh, you fool!" exclaimed his wife. "If we don't do it all four of us will starve. Is that what you want?"

She would give him no peace until he gave in.

Hansel and Gretel were so hungry that they could not sleep and consequently they heard everything the woman said.

Gretel started crying and said, "Oh Hansel, what are we going to do?"

"Hush now, Gretel," said Hansel. "Don't worry, I will find a way to get us out of trouble."

When his parents were asleep, Hansel got up, put on his clothes and slipped outside.

The moon was full and bright, and the little stones which lay in front of the house sparkled

like silver pieces. Hansel bent down and filled his pockets with as many of the pebbles as he could carry.

Then he went back inside and whispered to Gretel, "Sleep in peace, little sister. I have a plan which will save us." Then he went back to bed.

Early in the morning, an hour before sunrise, the woman roused the two children, shaking them roughly.

"Wake up, you lazy children. We all have to go to the forest to gather wood," she snapped.

Then she gave each of them a little piece of bread and said, "This is your breakfast, but don't eat it too soon because you won't get any more food today."

Gretel put the two pieces of bread in her apron because Hansel's pockets were full of stones, then they set off together to the forest.

Before they reached the wood, Hansel stopped to look back at the house. He did this so often that his father became curious.

"Why do you keep stopping to look at the house?" he asked. "Watch out you don't trip over your own legs!"

"I'm looking at my white cat," replied Hansel. "He's sitting on the top of the roof and wants to say goodbye to me."

"Fool!" said the woman. "That is not your little white cat, it is only the rising sun that shines on the chimney."

But of course, Hansel had really been lagging behind so that he could lay a trail with the stones which he had hidden in his pockets. One by one he dropped the pebbles on the ground.

When they arrived in the middle of the forest, their father said, "Now you two gather some wood and I will make you a fire so that you will not get cold."

Hansel and Gretel together did as he said and soon they had made a pile of firewood as tall as a little hill.

Their father lit the fire and when the flames were burning high his wife said, "Children, sit close by the fire and rest. We will go further into the forest to chop trees. When we have finished we will come back for you."

Hansel and Gretel sat near the fire and at midday they both ate their little pieces of bread. All the time they could hear the sound of an axe, so they thought that their father was not far away. But the noise did not come from an axe at all – it was only a branch which their father had fastened to a tree, blowing backwards and forwards in the wind.

At last the children's eyes closed with exhaustion and they fell sound asleep.

When they finally awoke it was already dark.

Gretel began to cry and said, "How will we find our way out of the forest?"

"Wait until the moon has risen," answered Hansel, hugging her, "then we will find our way back."

As soon as the moon rose, Hansel took his little sister by the hand and they followed the path of little stones which glittered like silver pieces and marked the way home.

It was almost daylight when they reached home.

They knocked at the door and, when the woman opened it and saw it was Hansel and

Gretel, she said, "You naughty children, where have you been all night? We thought you were lost."

Their father was delighted to see them and welcomed them into the house. But it wasn't long before, once again, the children overheard the woman complaining to their father.

"We only have half a loaf of bread and after that is finished there is nothing left to eat. We have to get rid of the children. We will take them even further into the forest so that they cannot find their way back. There is no other solution."

Their father was heartbroken and thought it would be better to share the last piece of bread with the children instead of sending them away, but the woman did not want to hear any more about it and started to scold him until at last he gave in again.

When their parents were asleep, Hansel got up and went to gather stones as he had done before, but this time the door was locked and Hansel could not go outside.

Nevertheless, he comforted his little sister and said, "Don't worry, I will find a way to get us out of trouble."

Early in the morning the woman got the children out of bed and gave them each a little piece of bread, even smaller than the last time.

While they walked to the forest, Hansel kept stopping to drop crumbs on the ground, crumbled from the bread he had in his pocket.

"Hansel, why do you keep lagging behind?" said his father. "Hurry up!"

"I am looking at my pigeon that is sitting on the top of the roof and wants to say goodbye to me," replied Hansel.

"You fool!" exclaimed the woman. "That is not your pigeon, it is only the rising sun lighting up the chimney."

Hansel continued to secretly drop breadcrumbs along the path.

Deeper and deeper into the forest they were taken, where they had never been before in their lives.

As before, their father lit a big fire for them and the woman said, "Stay here by the fire. We are going into the forest to chop trees and in the evening, when we are finished, we will come to take you home again."

At midday Gretel shared her piece of bread with Hansel, who had crumbled his piece along the road, then they went to sleep. They did not awake until it was dark and no one came to fetch them. Hansel comforted his little sister by saying:

"Wait, Gretel, until the moon has risen, then we will be able to see the crumbs I have scattered.

They will show us the way home."

When the moon rose they got up, but they could not find any crumbs because the birds that lived in the forest had eaten them all.

"Never mind, we will find the way back ourselves," said Hansel.

But they could not find it. They walked the entire night, and even the next day from sunrise to sunset, without finding their way out of the forest.

They were very hungry for they had not had

anything to eat other than a few wild strawberries that they had found growing by the path. At last they were so tired that their legs could not carry them any longer, so they lay down under a tree and fell asleep.

Next day they tried again to find their way home, but still they only went deeper and deeper into the forest.

Near midday, they saw a beautiful bird, as white as snow, perched on a branch and singing so beautifully that the children almost forgot their hunger as they stopped to listen.

Then the bird spread its wings and flew away. The children followed the bird to a little house. When they came closer they saw with amazement that the little house was made of gingerbread and cakes, and the windows were made of brown sugar.

"This is just what we need," said Hansel. "We will make a good meal from it. I am going to start with the roof. Gretel, why don't you try some of the window?"

Hansel climbed on to the roof and broke off a piece, while Gretel began to lick the windows.

Suddenly, a soft voice came from inside:

"Nibble, nibble, mouse!
Who is nibbling at my little house?"

And the children answered:

"The wind, the wind,
Only the wind."

They carried on eating without another thought as they were still very hungry. Hansel, who liked the taste of the roof, tore down a large piece of it, and Gretel pushed out an entire window-pane, which she then began to nibble.

Suddenly the door opened and an old, bent woman came creeping out. Hansel and Gretel were so frightened that they dropped their sweets.

The old woman nodded her head and said, "My dear children, however did you get here? Come inside and stay with me in my house – you will enjoy it here."

She took both children by the hand and led them into the little house. There she gave them a delicious meal – milk and pancakes with sugar,

apples and nuts. Then she prepared two little beds in which Hansel and Gretel were soon fast asleep, thinking they were in heaven.

Now this old woman seemed very friendly, but in reality she was a mean witch who caught and ate little children. She had built her little house of gingerbread to trap them, then she fed them until they were fat enough to eat.

This witch didn't have very good eyesight, but she had an excellent sense of smell. When she smelled Hansel and Gretel approaching the house,

she laughed an evil cackle and cried, "They will not escape!"

The next morning she woke Hansel, grabbed him with her shrivelled hand and took him to a small stable where she locked him up behind a door with bars for a window. Then she went back to Gretel and shook her until she awoke.

"Get up, you lazy child," she cried. "Go and get me some water so that I can cook something nice for your brother. He is in the stable and has to be fattened up. As soon as he is fat enough, I will eat him."

Gretel began to weep, but all in vain. She was forced to do what the witch had ordered. The witch then prepared Hansel some of the best food, but to Gretel she gave only crab shells.

Every morning the old woman crept into the stable and cried, "Hansel, stretch out your finger, so I can feel if you have become fat."

But Hansel stretched out a little bone he had found on the floor and, because the witch was short-sighted, she thought it was his finger and was surprised that he was not getting any fatter.

Four weeks passed by in this way. Hansel remained thin and eventually her impatience got

the better of her. One day she decided that she could not wait any longer.

"Hurry up, Gretel, bring me some water," she ordered the young girl. "Whether Hansel is fat or thin, I will kill him and cook him tomorrow."

Gretel wept and wept. "If the wild beasts in the forest had eaten us, we would at least have died together!" she sobbed.

"Spare me your whining," said the witch. "It will not help you in any way."

The following morning Gretel had to fill the big cooking pot with water and light the fire.

"First we will bake some bread," said the witch. "I have heated the oven and kneaded the dough."

She pushed poor Gretel towards the burning flames that came out of the oven.

"Creep inside to see whether it is warm enough, so that we can put the bread in."

Gretel guessed that once she was inside the witch would close the door and roast her to eat as well, so she scratched her head and pretended to look puzzled.

"I don't know how to get inside," she said.

"Oh you stupid goose!" said the witch. "The opening is big enough. You see, I even fit inside it myself."

She put her head into the oven door. Gretel immediately gave a great shove and pushed the old witch right inside the hot oven. Then she shut the iron door and fastened the bolt. That soon put an end to the evil witch!

Gretel ran quickly to Hansel, opened the stable door and cried, "Hansel, we are free! The old witch is dead!"

How they danced with joy and hugged each other. Then, as they had nothing to be afraid of any longer, they went through the entire house

where they found all sorts of precious pearls and stones.

Laughing, the two children gathered up as much treasure as they could carry. Hansel filled his pockets and Gretel filled her apron.

"Now, let's go quickly. I'm sure we will now be able to find our way out of this bewitched forest," said Hansel.

After they had walked through the forest for an hour or two the children arrived at a great river.

"We will not be able to get over to the other side," said Hansel. "I don't see a bridge or raft."

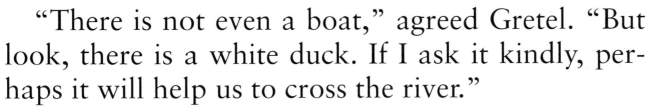

"There is not even a boat," agreed Gretel. "But look, there is a white duck. If I ask it kindly, perhaps it will help us to cross the river."

And she cried:

> "Little duck, little duck, do you see,
> Hansel and Gretel are waiting for thee?
> There's never a plank, or bridge in sight,
> Take us across on your back so white."

The duck swam towards them right away and Hansel seated himself on its back.

He wanted his sister to sit next to him.

"No," said Gretel. "Both of us will be too heavy for the duck. It will take us across, one by one."

When they were both safely on the other side of the river they started walking again. As they walked, the forest became more familiar and the children began to see things that they recognized.

At last they gave a glad cry as they saw the clearing where their own home was.

Then the children began to run; they burst into the house and flung their arms around their father's neck.

59

The man was overjoyed to see his children safe and sound. He had not known one happy hour since he had left them behind in the forest and his wife was now dead.

Gretel emptied her apron pocket and the pearls and precious stones rolled around the room. Hansel threw one handful of jewels after another out of his pocket.

At last all their worries were over. From that day on the family never knew a hungry day and they all lived together in perfect happiness.

The Little Match Girl

It was the last night of the year, New Year's Eve. and it was so terribly cold! It was snowing, and soon it would be dark.

Through the cold and the darkness, a poor little girl wandered in the street, with bare feet and no scarf for her head. She had, indeed, worn slippers when she left home, but they were not much use. They were very big slippers that her mother had worn before her. They were so big that the little girl had lost them rushing to cross the street in between two carts.

One of the slippers was nowhere to be found, and the other was taken by a boy who intended to use it as a cradle when he had children of his own.

The little girl wandered along in her bare feet which were blue with cold. She was carrying several matches in her old apron and was holding one bundle in her hand. It had been a bad day for her; no one had bought any matches and she had not earned a single penny. She was very hungry and very cold, and looked very frail. Poor little girl!

Lights were glittering from all the windows and there was a wonderful smell of roasting meat along the whole street. All the little girl could think of was that it was New Year's Eve. She sat

down and tried to warm herself in a corner between two houses. She grew colder and colder, but she did not dare to go home for she would have to take back all the matches, but not one penny. Her father would beat her and, besides, it would be cold at home as well. They only lived in a little hut and the wind blew right through it, even though the biggest cracks had been stuffed with straw and rags.

Her little hands were almost dead with cold. A lighted match would at least do some good! Maybe she would dare to take just one out of the

bundle, strike it against the wall, and warm her fingers!

And so she took one. Whoosh! How it sparkled! How it burned! It was a gentle warm flame, just like a little candle when she held her hand around it. But what a strange light! It seemed to the little girl as if she were sitting in front of a huge iron stove with polished brass knobs and gleaming pots and pans. The fire was magnificent and gave out so much warmth! The child had just stretched her feet out to warm them, when the flame went out and the stove disappeared. She was sitting there with only a little burnt match-end in her hand.

The girl struck another match which burned and glowed, and where the light fell on the wall it became transparent like gauze. The child could see into a room where a table was covered with a white cloth and set with fine china. There was a roast goose, stuffed with prunes and apples, which filled the room with a delicious smell. What a surprise! Suddenly the goose jumped from its plate and rolled on the floor, straight to the poor girl, with the fork and knife still in its back.

Then the match went out and there was nothing

to see but the thick, cold wall.

She struck a third match. Immediately she found herself sitting under a magnificent Christmas tree. It was even bigger and more beautifully decorated than the one she had seen through the glass doors at the rich merchant's house last Christmas. A thousand candles were burning on the green branches, and it seemed as if all the colorful figures were smiling at her. The little girl held up both hands and the match went out. The Christmas candles rose higher and higher, and she then realized they were just stars. One of them fell and made a long streak of fire in the sky.

"Someone is dying," whispered the little girl, for her old grandmother, who was the only one who had ever been kind to her, but who had died, used to say to her: "If you see a falling star it means that a soul is going up to heaven."

She struck another match against the wall which made a great light. This time in the middle of that brightness she saw her grandmother. She looked so sweet and so shining.

"Oh Granny, take me with you," cried the girl. "When the match goes out, I know you won't be there any longer. You will disappear just like the

iron stove, the roasted goose and the beautiful Christmas tree."

She suddenly struck the rest of the bundle because she wanted to keep her grandmother, and the matches shone so gloriously that it was brighter than daylight. Never before had her grandmother seemed so tall and so beautiful. She took the little girl in her arms and they both flew away in radiant joy, higher and higher until there was no more cold, no more hunger and no more suffering. They were in Paradise.

In the cold, early morning, the little girl was still sitting in the corner between the two houses. Her cheeks were red and she had a smile on her lips… She was dead, frozen to death on New Year's Eve.

New Year's morning rose over her little body sitting there with the matches, one bundle almost completely burnt up.

"She just wanted to keep herself warm!" someone said.

But no one knew what beautiful things she had seen, nor in what radiance she had entered the New Year with her old grandmother.

Puss in Boots

Once there was a miller who, when he died, had nothing to leave his children but his mill, his donkey and his cat. The property was soon divided, without involving a lawyer or a judge since their fees would have taken the whole meager inheritance. The eldest son had the mill, the second son had the donkey and the youngest had only the cat.

The third son was not happy with such a small inheritance.

"My brothers can earn an honest living by

working together," he said. "But as for me, once I have eaten the cat and made myself a scarf out of his skin, what shall I do?"

The cat overheard his speech and drew himself up in a dignified manner.

"Don't worry, my master. You only need to give me a drawstring bag, and have a pair of boots made for me so that I can go through thick undergrowth, and you will see that you are not half as badly off as you thought."

Although the cat's master did not have much confidence in this promise, he decided he would try anything to escape being poor. And, after all, he had seen his cat perform cunning tricks in order to catch rats and mice.

When the cat was given what he had asked for, he put on the boots. Then he put some grain and lettuce in the bag, slung the bag over his shoulder and set off for a den where he knew there was a large number of rabbits. There he stretched out on the ground as if he were dead and then waited for some young innocent rabbit to go into his bag to eat the bait.

He had no sooner lain down, when his plan worked. A young rabbit was tempted into the bag,

where the clever cat trapped it by immediately pulling the drawstrings. Very proud of his catch, he went to the palace to seek an audience with the king.

He was taken to His Majesty's room where he bowed deeply and said, "Majesty, here is a wild rabbit I am commanded to present to you in the name of the Marquis de Carabas." (This was the name he had made up for his master.)

"Tell your master that I am very pleased and that I thank him," replied the king.

A few days later the cat hid in a wheat field and set his trap again. When two partridges wandered into the bag he pulled the strings and caught them both. Then he went to the king, as he had done with the wild rabbit. The king accepted the two partridges with great pleasure and gave the cat something to drink.

The cat continued in this way for two or three months, visiting the king from time to time to take him game supposedly from his master's hunting.

One day when he heard that the king was going for a drive along the river bank with his daughter, the most beautiful princess in the world, the cat said to his master, "If you would follow my

advice, your fortune is made. You only have to bathe in the river at the place I will show you and then let me do the rest."

The young man did what his cat advised him, although he wondered what good it would do him.

While he was bathing, the king passed by and the cat started to shout at the top of his voice, "Help! Help! My master, the Marquis de Carabas is drowning here!"

When the king heard this cry he put his head out of the carriage window and recognized the cat who had brought him game so many times. He ordered his guards to rescue the Marquis.

While the poor young man was being pulled out of the river, the cat approached the carriage and told the king that some wicked thieves had stolen his master's clothes. (The cat had, in fact, hidden them under a big stone!) The king immediately ordered his Master of the Wardrobe to pick out one of his most beautiful suits for the Marquis de Carabas.

The king paid the young man a lot of attention, and the beautiful clothes that were given to him emphasized his handsome face and figure. The

king's daughter admired him a great deal; indeed, it wasn't long before she was completely in love with him. The king invited the marquis to get into the carriage to join them for the rest of the trip.

The cat was delighted to see that his plan had started to work, but there was still a great deal to do. He ran on ahead and soon came across some farmers cutting hay in a meadow.

"Listen farmers," he said, "if you do not tell the king that the field you are working in belongs to the Marquis de Carabas, you will all be chopped up as fine as meat for hamburgers.

Sure enough, when the king arrived he asked the farmers whose field they were working on.

"It belongs to the Marquis de Carabas," they all replied.

"You have a considerable inheritance there," said the king to the Marquis de Carabas.

"As you see, Majesty, it is a meadow which provides for an abundant crop every single year," answered the young man, although he had been truly astonished by their words.

The ingenious cat, still walking ahead, next encountered some harvesters, and told them, "Listen harvesters, if you do not say that all this

wheat belongs to the Marquis de Carabas you will be ground up as fine as meat for hamburgers."

The king, who passed by a moment later, asked to whom all the wheat belonged.

"It belongs to the Marquis de Carabas," answered the harvesters, and the king was even more delighted with the young man.

The cat, who walked well ahead of the carriage, kept on saying the same thing to everyone he encountered, and the king was astonished to see the immense wealth of the Marquis de Carabas.

Finally the artful cat arrived at a beautiful castle belonging to an ogre; indeed, all the land the king had been driving through was part of the estate of this castle. The cat knew this and asked to speak to the ogre. The ogre received him as courteously as an ogre can, and asked him to sit down.

"I have been informed," said the cat, "that you possess the gift of being able to change yourself into all sorts of animals; that you could transform yourself, for example, into a lion or an elephant?"

"That is true," answered the ogre brusquely, "and just to show you, I will change into a lion."

The cat was so terrified to see a lion before him that he jumped for the nearest rafter to reach the

79

safety of the roof, but the boots he was wearing made it difficult and dangerous.

When the ogre had changed back again, he came down and licked his ruffled fur.

"I have also been informed," continued the cat, "that you also have the power to take the form of smaller animals. For example, that you can change yourself into a rat or a mouse. I find this almost impossible to believe."

"Impossible? Wait and see!" exclaimed the ogre. At once he changed himself into a mouse and started running across the floor.

The cat no sooner saw the mouse, than he pounced, caught and ate it!

In the meantime, the king had arrived at the ogre's castle and wanted to call on the owner. Hearing the sound of the carriage rumbling across the drawbridge, the cat ran towards it and said to the king, "Your Majesty, welcome to the castle of the Marquis de Carabas."

"What! Monsieur le Marquis!" cried the king. "The castle also belongs to you?! I have never seen anything more beautiful than this courtyard and all the buildings around it. Let us see inside, please."

The young man gave the princess his hand and followed the king into a large room where a magnificent meal was laid out. The ogre had had this meal prepared for his friends who should have been visiting him that day, but who had not dared to approach the castle knowing the king was there.

Both the king and his daughter were quite charmed by the excellent qualities of the Marquis de Carabas. Having also seen all the wealth the marquis possessed, the king at last said to him, "I see no reason why, if you agree, you should not be my son-in-law, Monsieur le Marquis."

The Marquis, bowing low, accepted the honor the king did him; and that very day he married the princess.

The clever cat was given the title 'Great Lord' and never again ran after mice, except for fun!

All's Well That Ends Well

I will tell you a story that I heard when I was a little boy. Each time I recall the end of the story it seems to get better; in fact, there are some stories like some people – they seem to get more beautiful as they grow older.

Once there were two very old farms, each with thatched roofs covered with grass and moss, and each with a stork's nest on the roof. The walls leaned to the right and to the left; there were only two or three low windows and all of them were stuck fast, but one. The oven stuck out of the wall

like a fat tummy. A honeysuckle grew out of the hedge, and under its branches was a duck pond. A watchdog barked at everyone passing by.

In one of these cottages lived an old couple – a farmer and his wife. They possessed almost nothing in the world, except for a horse which ate grass from the ditches at the side of the road. The farmer always rode the horse when he went to the city. His neighbors often borrowed the horse and, in return, they helped the good man with all kinds of jobs. However, he thought that it would be better to get rid of the horse. He decided to sell it or exchange it for something that would be even more useful to them, whatever it might be.

"Something you appreciate more than anyone else does," said his wife. "Today there is a fair in the city. Go there with the horse. You will make a profit by selling it, or you can exchange it for something else. Anything you do is fine with me: so get ready to go!"

She put a beautiful scarf around his neck which she tied with a very stylish double knot. She smoothed out his hat with the palm of her hand and gave him a big kiss. Then he rode off into town on the horse, to sell or exchange it.

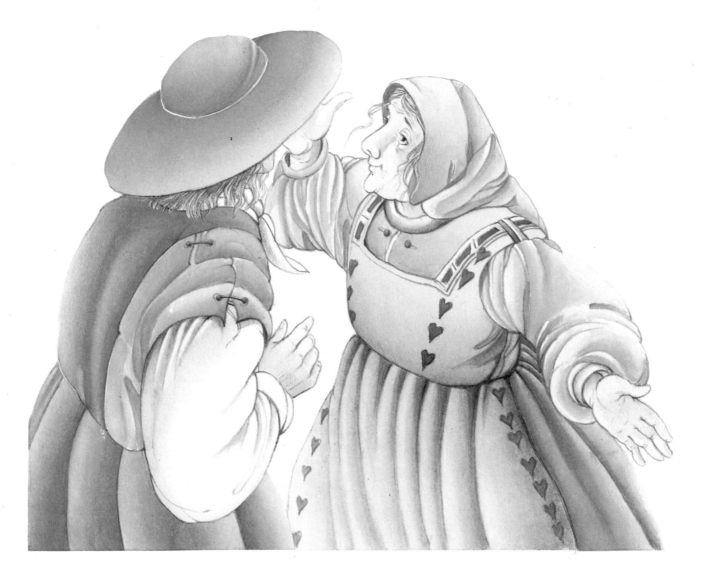

"Yes, the old man knows what he is doing. He knows how to do business better than anyone else," said his wife, as she waved goodbye.

The sun was blazing and there was not a cloud in the sky. The wind blew up the dust from the road along which all kinds of people hurried to get to the city, by cart, on horse or on foot. They were all very hot, but there was no inn to be seen.

Among these people walked a man leading a

cow to the market. It was as beautiful as a cow can be.

"She must give delicious milk!" thought the farmer. "Now, that would be a splendid exchange – that superb cow in return for my horse!"

He called out, "Hey, you there, the man with the cow! I have an offer for you. A horse, I know, costs much more than a cow, but that makes no difference to me – a cow will give me more profit than a horse. Would you like to exchange your cow for my horse?"

"I would be delighted!" answered the man, and they exchanged their animals.

Well, that had been taken care of, and the old farmer could have returned home because he had finished the business he had set out to do. But because he had looked forward to seeing the fair he decided to go to the city anyway. He continued the journey with his cow and, as he was walking briskly, it wasn't long before he joined up with another man leading a sheep of a rare breed, with a thick woolly fleece.

"Now, there is a beautiful animal I would like to have!" said the farmer to himself. "A sheep will find all the grass it needs along our hedges. During

the winter we can keep it in the house – that will be a nice distraction for my dear wife. A sheep will be better for us than a cow."

He called to the owner of the sheep, "Hello friend, would you like to swap?"

The man did not need to be asked twice. He rushed to take the cow and left the sheep behind.

The old farmer continued his journey with the sheep. A little further on he saw a man carrying a live goose under his arm. It was a fine fat goose – a goose that you wouldn't find just anywhere. The old farmer admired it.

"Now, there you have a nice creature," he said walking up to the man. "That bird is extraordinary – so much fat! And such beautiful feathers!"

The farmer couldn't stop thinking about that goose! "If it lived at our house, I bet my dear wife would find a way of making it even fatter. We could give it all the left-overs; what a size it would get! I remember my wife often saying, 'Ah! If we had a goose, that would be so nice, together with all our ducks!' This is perhaps the chance to get one, and one that is worth two!"

"Listen, my friend," he said. "Would you like to trade with me? Take my sheep and give me your

goose in return? I ask for nothing more."

This man did not have to be asked twice either, and the old farmer became the owner of the goose. By this time he was close to the city. The crowd became bigger; men and animals hurried along the road. There were even people walking in the ditches along the field hedges. At the fair gate everyone pushed to get in.

The city's tax collector held up a chicken. Seeing such a crowd, he fastened the chicken on a string so that it could not get frightened and run away. She perched on the gate and ruffled her clipped wings; she winked with her eye like a mischievous animal, and said: "cluck, cluck".

Was she thinking about something? I wouldn't know, but the farmer began to laugh as soon as he noticed her.

"She is even more beautiful than the pastor's brood hen," he chuckled. "And she looks so funny! No one could look at her without bursting into laughter! Goodness! I would love to have her. A chicken is the easiest animal to keep. She doesn't have to be looked after. She would feed herself with grain and crumbs picked from the ground. I think that if I could exchange my goose

for her, I would make an excellent deal."

He approached the tax collector. "Would you like to exchange?" he said, showing him his goose.

"Exchange!" answered the man. "That would be perfect!"

The tax collector accepted the goose and the old farmer took the chicken. The farmer had done quite a bit of business during the journey and now he was very hot and tired. He needed something to drink and to eat, so he went into an inn. A boy was just leaving carrying a bag filled to the brim.

"What are you carrying there?" asked the farmer.

"A bag of stunted apples that I am going to feed to the pigs," replied the boy.

"What did you say? Stunted apples for the pigs? But that is a wasteful extravagance! My dear wife does great things with stunted apples. How happy she would be with all those! Last year, our old apple tree next to the stables did not give a single fruit. We will place them in the cupboard and save them until they have ripened. 'That is a sign that one feels comfortable,' my wife always says. What will she say if she has a bag full of apples? I would love to do her that favor."

"Well, what would you give in return for the bag?" asked the boy.

"What I would give you! The chicken of course! Isn't that enough?" said the farmer.

They exchanged their goods straight away and the farmer walked into the inn with his bag which he carefully placed beside the stove. Then he had a drink. The stove was hot, but the farmer did not notice.

There were many people in the inn – horse traders, cattlemen and also two French travellers. The Frenchmen were so rich that their pockets were chock-full with gold pieces. And how they loved to bet, as you will see!

Ssss-ssss! Suddenly the stove began to make a strange noise. It was the apples starting to cook.

"What is that?" asked one of the Frenchmen.

"Ah, my apples!" said the farmer, and he told the Frenchmen the story of the horse that he had traded for a cow, and so on, until he was left with the apples.

"Eh well, she will be furious, your missus, when you go home!" they said.

"Not at all!" said the farmer. "She will embrace me no matter what happens, and she will say:

'What the old man does is always right. All's well that ends well'."

"You want to bet?" said the Frenchmen. "We will bet all the gold you want – a hundred pounds worth, or a hundred kilos."

"One satchel will be enough," replied the farmer. "The only thing I can place as a bet in return is my bag of apples. I'd say that is a good exchange. What do you think gentlemen?"

"All right, that's good enough; we accept!"

So the bet was made. The three men borrowed the innkeeper's cart, climbed into it and very soon

they arrived at the little rustic farm.

"Good evening, my dear," said the farmer, entering the cottage.

"Good evening to you, my darling," replied his wife.

"I have exchanged the horse."

"Ah! You know how to do business," said the woman, and she embraced him without paying any attention to the bag of apples or the strangers.

"I exchanged the horse for a cow," said the farmer.

"Thank Heavens! The good milk we will have, and butter and cheese! That is a wonderful exchange," cried his wife.

"Yes, but then I traded the cow for a sheep," continued the farmer.

"Well, that is even better," smiled his wife. "We have enough grass to feed the sheep and she will give us milk too. I love sheep cheese. And above all that, I will have wool which I can use to knit stockings and nice warm jackets. Oh, we wouldn't get all that from a cow. You think of everything!"

"This is not the end yet, my dear. I exchanged this sheep for a goose."

"Well then, we will have a lovely roast goose

for Christmas this year! My dear husband, you always think about what would please me the most. Well done! From now until Christmas we will have time to make it nice and fat."

"I don't have this goose any more; I have taken a chicken in return," continued the farmer.

"A chicken has its value," nodded his wife. "A chicken lays eggs, she sits on them, and little chicks will hatch out that grow up and soon we will have poultry. A real farmyard – that has always been my dream."

"It is not there any more, dear wife. I exchanged it for a bag of stunted apples," finished the farmer.

"Really? Is that true?" gasped his wife. "But now I will kiss you, my dear husband! Do you want to hear what happened this morning? You had just left and I began to think about what I could make for you for dinner tonight. Eggs with butter and onions was the best I think of. Well, I had the eggs and the butter, but I didn't have any onions.

"So I went to the school principal who grows them and I talked to his wife. You know how mean she is, although she looks so sweet? I begged her to lend me a handful of onions. 'Lend!' she exclaimed. 'But we don't have anything in our garden – no onions, not even any stunted apples. I am really sorry, my neighbor.'

"So I came home again. Tomorrow I will offer her the stunted apples because she doesn't have any. I will offer her the whole bag! She will be so embarrassed! I'm looking forward to seeing her face already!"

She flung her arms around her husband's neck and gave him smacking kisses, almost as if she were kissing a child.

"Well, well!" said the two Frenchmen. "The fall in value has not changed her good mood for even a second. I think you have won your bet, friend!"

They gave the farmer a satchel of gold. His wife was even more delighted with it after all that bargaining, and the man was suddenly richer than if he had sold his horse ten times, at thirty times its value.

That is the story that I was told when I was a little child, and it seems very sensible to me. Now you know it as well, and never forget it: "What the old man does is always right, and all's well that ends well!"

The Princess
and the Pea

Once upon a time there was a prince who wanted to marry a princess, but she had to be a real princess. So he travelled around the world to find one. There were a great many princesses, but he was never sure whether they truly were real princesses. There was always something not quite right about them. At last he returned home very unhappy because he could not find what he was looking for.

One evening there was a terrible storm with thunder and lightning, and rain pouring down in

torrents. It was dreadful! Suddenly, there was a loud knocking at the castle door and the king hurried to open it.

There on the doorstep was a princess. But what a sight! She was drenched. Water ran down from her hair and her clothes; it ran down into the tops of her shoes and out of the toes. Nevertheless, she insisted that she was a real princess.

"We will soon find out!" thought the queen, eyeing the bedraggled girl. However, she said nothing and went to prepare a bedroom for the unexpected guest. She stripped all the bedding off and placed a pea on the base of the bed. Then she took twenty mattresses and laid them on the pea, after which she then laid twenty eiderdown quilts on top of that.

Then the queen showed the princess where she had to spend the night and the girl climbed in thankfully.

The next morning the king and queen asked her how she had slept.

"Oh, terribly badly!" she said, "I hardly shut my eyes the whole night! Goodness knows what was in the bed. It was something very hard, and now I am black and blue all over."

By this answer the queen knew she was a real princess. Only a princess would be sensitive enough to feel a pea through twenty mattresses and twenty eiderdown quilts.

The prince at long last had found his real princess whom he married, and the pea was placed in the museum where it can still be seen today – if it has not been stolen.

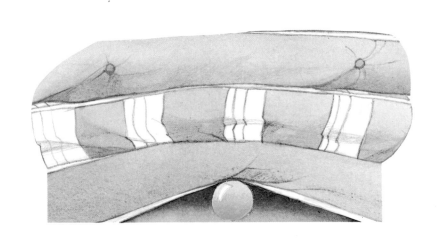

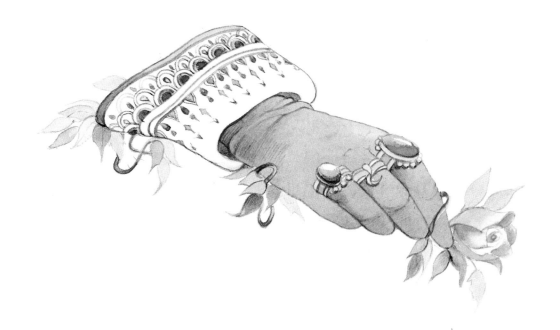

Beauty and the Beast

Once upon a time there was a rich merchant. He had six children – three boys and three girls.

His daughters were very beautiful, but the youngest was admired the most. She was called Beauty because the name suited her, which made her sisters green with envy. And if this were not enough, she was also more intelligent than her sisters.

One day the merchant lost everything he owned, except for a little cottage far away from the city. In tears he told his children that they

would have to move to the cottage and that, from now on, they would have to make a living by farming.

And so they moved into the cottage, and the merchant and his three sons became farmers and learned to work the land.

Each morning Beauty would wake up at four o'clock and hurry to clean the house and make breakfast for the family. When she had finished the housework she spent her time reading, playing the harpsichord or singing.

In contrast, her two sisters were always bored. They didn't wake until ten o'clock in the morning; then they would go for long walks and pass their time talking about all the friends and beautiful clothes they'd once had. They looked with scorn and jealousy on Beauty's simple pleasures.

"Look at our youngest sister," they said to each other. "She is so stupid that she is happy in her misery."

When they had been in the cottage for about a year the merchant received a letter telling him of a ship which would make his fortune. In haste he made ready to travel on the long journey to the port.

The good news made the two elder sisters excited. When their father was ready to leave they danced around him and begged him to bring them new dresses and all kinds of presents. Beauty, however, said nothing.

"Don't you want me to buy you anything?" asked her father.

"There is nothing I really need," she said, "but, since you are so kind as to ask, would you please bring me back a rose if you should see one on your travels? There are no bushes to be found in

these parts and they are the one thing that I have truly missed since we have been here."

And so their father left, but when he arrived at the port he found that the ship's cargo was worthless and he had to return home just as poor as he had been before.

Sadly he started the long journey back, disappointed that he could not even afford one present for his children.

He was only about thirty miles from home when disaster struck once more. While riding through a vast forest he somehow missed his way and became lost. It began to snow heavily and the wind was so strong that he was twice thrown from his horse. When darkness came he was sure he would starve of hunger or cold, or that he would be eaten by the howling wolves.

Suddenly he saw a light at the end of a long tree-lined path. It seemed quite far away but just the thought of shelter gave the merchant a little strength.

He walked towards it and saw that the light came from a brightly lit palace. Astonished, he passed through the gateway; the courtyard was quite empty.

His horse, which followed him, saw an empty stable and went inside. The cold, starving animal found some hay and oats which it started to eat greedily, while the merchant walked to the house.

Still he found no one, but when he entered a large hall, there he found a welcoming fire blazing in the fireplace and a table full of food, set for just one person.

The merchant was soaked to the skin so he went to the fireplace to dry himself off.

"The master of the house will forgive me for making myself at home," he thought. "He will probably arrive soon and I can explain."

He waited for quite a long time, but when still no one had arrived by eleven o'clock he could no longer resist his hunger and helped himself to a chicken which he ate in two bites. Then he drank a couple of glasses of wine which made him very sleepy.

He left the hall and passed through several huge corridors, all magnificently decorated. At the end of one he found a bedroom in which there was a comfortable bed. The sight of it was too much for the tired man; without thinking further, he threw himself into it and fell fast asleep.

The merchant slept well and did not wake up until ten o'clock the next morning. When he got up and looked for his clothes he was very surprised to find that they had been replaced by brand-new ones.

After a magnificent breakfast he went outside to find his horse.

On the way he walked under a rose-covered archway and, remembering Beauty's request, he picked a branch on which there grew several roses.

"At least one of my dear children will have a gift," he smiled to himself.

Suddenly he heard a terrible noise and saw a beast coming towards him, a monster so horrible that he almost fainted in terror.

"You ungrateful wretch," roared the Beast. "I saved your life by letting you into my palace, and you reward me by stealing my roses which I love more than anything in the world. Now you will die!"

The merchant fell to his knees and begged the Beast not to harm him.

"Forgive me, Sir, I did not think you would be offended if I picked a rose for one of my daughters

who wanted one so badly."

"Don't call me Sir. I am known as the Beast," answered the creature. "I prefer it that people say what they think, so don't think your flattery will change anything.

"However, I will forgive you on condition that one of your daughters comes here willingly to die in your place. If your daughters refuse to die for you, you must return to me in three months and receive your punishment."

The man had no intention of sacrificing one of his daughters to the evil monster, but he said to himself, "At least I will have the chance to embrace them one more time before I die."

So he promised that he would return and, fetching his horse, he left the palace.

A few hours later the man arrived home, tired and sad.

His children ran towards him with open arms, but the merchant looked at them with tears in his eyes. In his hand he held the branch of roses he brought for Beauty.

He gave it to her and said, "Take these roses; your unhappy father has indeed paid a great price for them."

Then he told his family all about the worthless ship, the magical palace and the misfortune that had befallen him.

After hearing his story, his two older daughters started to cry.

But Beauty said, "There is no need for our father to die. I will willingly offer myself to the Beast in his place."

"No, my sister," said her three brothers. "We will track down the monster and kill him first. Surely all three of us can defeat him."

"My children," said the merchant, "this Beast is too powerful even for you. Besides, the Beast saved my life, although he now intends to take it. I gave my word: I am old and will not regret losing the last few years of my life, thanks to you, my dear children."

"I assure you, my father, that you will not go to the palace without me," said Beauty. "You can't stop me from following you. I would rather be eaten by this monster than die of a broken heart from losing you."

Her father and brothers begged and pleaded with her, but there was nothing they could say to make her change her mind.

The two elder daughters rubbed their eyes with an onion and pretended to cry when Beauty left with her father. Her brothers and her father also wept, but Beauty didn't cry at all because she did not want to make her family even more miserable.

They rode the horse to the palace and, as darkness fell, found it as brightly lit as before.

The horse found shelter in the stable and the man entered the large hall with his daughter, where they found a table magnificently laid out and set for two.

Beauty thought to herself, "The Beast wants to

fatten me up before he eats me."

After dinner they heard a great roaring. Beauty could hardly stop herself from fainting in terror when she saw the horrible monster, but she tried to control her fear and, when the Beast asked her if she had come of her own choice, she told him with a trembling voice that she had.

"You are very kind," said the Beast, "and I am very grateful that you decided to come."

He then turned to the man and said to him, "Say goodbye to your daughter. You will leave here tomorrow morning and never come back. Now, goodnight, Beauty!"

"Goodnight, Beast," she answered, and the monster disappeared.

That night, while she slept, Beauty dreamed of a fairy who told her, "I like and admire your kind heart, Beauty. The good deed you have done will be rewarded."

When Beauty woke up she told her father of her dream. Although this comforted him a little, it did not stop him from weeping bitterly when he had to leave his daughter.

When he had gone, Beauty sat down in the large hall and began to weep herself, thinking that the

Beast must surely eat her that night. Then, pulling herself together, she decided to explore.

She was very surprised when she came to a door with a sign that read, 'Beauty's Room'. She opened it and was impressed by what she saw: a large library, a harpsichord and several books about music.

On a shelf was a book inscribed in gold letters, 'Wish, command: here you are the queen and the mistress'.

"Alas!" she sighed. "I only wish I could see my poor father to know what he is doing at this very moment."

To her surprise, in the mirror she saw a vision of her father arriving home, looking very sad. All too soon the vision disappeared, but Beauty was no longer scared because she believed the Beast didn't mean to eat her after all.

At noon she found the table set with food for her. During the meal she could hear beautiful music, although she never saw anyone playing.

In the afternoon Beauty walked in the palace gardens. She felt quite safe, but that evening, as she sat at the table, she heard the noise of the Beast arriving and could not help shivering.

"Beauty, would you mind if I watched you have your dinner?" he asked.

"You are the master," answered Beauty trembling.

"Yes, but you are the only mistress here," assured the Beast. "You only have to tell me if I bore you and I will leave at once. Tell me, don't you think I am very ugly?"

"I admit that is true because I can't lie," said Beauty. "But I think that you are very kind."

"But that doesn't change my dreadful ugliness," said the monster." I know very well that I am just a beast."

"One is only a beast if one thinks it," Beauty assured him, kindly. "Only fools are not aware of that."

"Enjoy your meal, Beauty," said the monster. "Everything in this house is yours and I would be sad if you were unhappy."

"You are very kind," said Beauty, "and I appreciate your generosity."

"Oh yes, Beauty!" answered the Beast. "I have a good heart, but I am still a monster."

Beauty enjoyed her meal. She was no longer afraid of the monster, but she was very shocked

when he suddenly said, "Beauty, will you marry
me?"

She waited a moment before answering. She
feared that if she refused the monster would be
angry.

At last she told him with a trembling voice,
"No, Beast."

The poor monster wanted to sigh, but instead
he made a dreadful hissing noise that echoed
through the whole palace.

Then he sadly said, "Goodnight Beauty."

He left the room, sadly looking over his shoulder before he closed the door.

Beauty felt sorry for the poor Beast.

"Alas!" she said. "He is so kind, but I could never love a Beast."

Beauty spent three very happy months in the palace. Every evening the Beast would visit her and talk to her while she had dinner.

Every day, Beauty discovered new virtues in the monster and she became quite fond of him.

Just one thing troubled her; at night, before the monster went to bed he always asked her if she would become his wife, and every time he seemed to be overcome with pain when she refused.

One day she said to him, "You make me sad, Beast. I will always be your friend, but I could never marry you."

"If that is how it has to be," said the Beast, "I deserve what I get. I know very well I am horrible to look at. Nevertheless, promise me that you will never leave me."

These words embarrassed Beauty. She was missing her father a great deal and, although she could see a vision of him in the mirror any time she liked, she dearly wished to be able to speak to him

again and assure him that she was alive and well. She could also see how much he was missing her.

"I could promise never to leave you, but I would so much like to see my father once more. I would die of a broken heart if you were to refuse me this wish," said Beauty.

"I would rather die myself, than to make you unhappy," replied the monster. "But if I send you to your father you will stay there, and your poor Beast will die of heartbreak."

"No," answered Beauty. "I promise that I will return within a week. Your mirror has shown me that my sisters have married and that my brothers are now soldiers. My father is all alone – allow me to visit him for a week."

"You will be there tomorrow morning," said the Beast, giving her a jewelled ring. "Remember your promise. When you want to return you only have to put this magic ring on a table and go to sleep. Farewell, Beauty."

Having said this the Beast sighed as usual and Beauty went sadly to sleep, feeling guilty that she had hurt his feelings.

When she woke up the next morning she was in her father's house. He was beside himself with joy

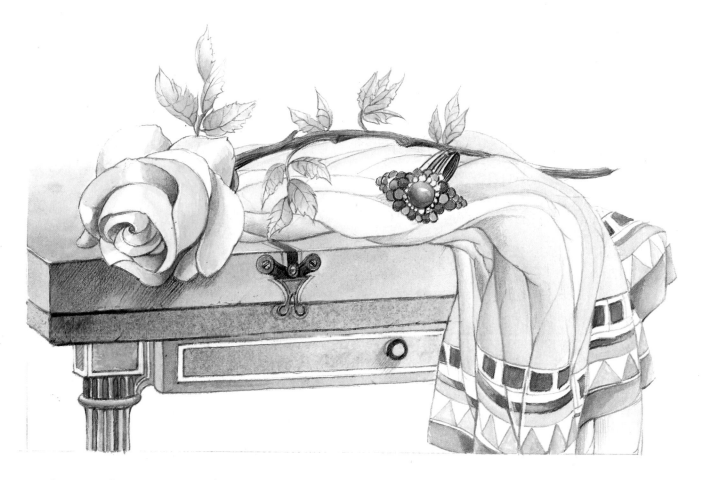

when he saw his sweet daughter again, and they
embraced each other for a very long time.

When Beauty's sisters heard the news they
rushed to the house with their husbands. They
were furious when they saw her dressed like a
princess and more beautiful than ever.

She was very sweet to them, but nothing could
stop them from being jealous.

The two girls went to the garden to grumble
together.

"Listen my sister," said the eldest. "I have an

idea. Let's try to make her stay here longer than a week. Her stupid Beast will be angry because she didn't keep her promise and maybe he will tear her to shreds."

"You are right, my sister," answered the other. "Let us be very sweet to her."

When a week had passed the two sisters begged so prettily for Beauty to stay that she promised to remain one more week.

Yet Beauty blamed herself for the grief she must be causing the poor Beast and, indeed, she even found that she missed his company.

The tenth night she spent at her father's house, she dreamt that she was in the palace garden. She saw the Beast stretched out on the grass – he was dying of a broken heart because she had not returned to him.

Beauty woke up in shock and began to weep.

"How could I break a Beast's heart who is so sweet to me!" she cried. "Is it his fault that he is so ugly, and has no hope? He is kind, and that is more important than anything else. I could never forgive myself if he died for my ingratitude."

So Beauty got up, put her magic ring on the table, and went back to sleep.

When she woke up the next morning she was delighted to find that she was back in the Beast's palace.

She dressed herself quickly, then spent all that day waiting for the Beast to arrive. She waited and waited, until the clock struck nine, but the Beast did not appear.

Beauty then feared the worst. She ran through the palace, searching desperately for the Beast. After she'd looked everywhere, she suddenly remembered her dream and ran out to the garden where she had seen him lying.

There she found the Beast unconscious on the ground and she thought he was dead.

She threw herself on him without a thought for his ugliness and felt his heart still beating, although only just. She took some water from the pond and threw it on his face.

At last the Beast opened his eyes and said, "You did not keep your promise, Beauty! But now I will die happily because I have had the chance to see you one more time."

Once more he closed his eyes and Beauty stroked his forehead.

"No, my dear Beast, you will not die," she said.

"You will live to become my husband; from this moment I will give you my hand in marriage, and I promise I will never leave you again. The pain I felt when I could not find you made me realize that I truly love you and I could not live without you."

Beauty looked at her dear Beast. But, what a surprise! The Beast had disappeared and at her feet she found the most handsome prince she had ever seen.

He got to his feet and stretched, then thanked

her for breaking his spell.

Although she had no eyes for anyone except the prince, Beauty could not stop herself from asking him where the Beast had gone.

"You see him here before you," the prince told her. "An evil fairy changed me into the Beast until the day that a beautiful girl agreed to marry me of her own free will. While I was under the spell I was forbidden to tell any girl the true story. It was hopeless, for who would want to marry a fearsome beast?

"You were the only one in the world with the heart to give me the chance to show my kind and gentle character and, by offering you my crown, I now also show you my gratitude and sincerity. You already know that I love you."

Beauty, who was amazed, took the handsome prince by the hand. They went into the palace together and Beauty was happier than ever when she saw her father and the rest of her family in the large hall. The fairy who had appeared in her dream had brought them to the palace and she, too, was there, smiling.

"Beauty, at last you have received your reward for making the right decision," said the good fairy.

"You have put virtue above beauty, and you deserve this prince who has such qualities himself. You will become a great queen and I have no fear that you will rule wisely and well."

Then the fairy turned to Beauty's two sisters.

"I know your evil hearts," she said. "You will become two stone statues that will stand at your sister's palace gate. All you will do each day is to witness her happiness, and there you will stay until the moment you admit your mistakes. However, I am afraid that you may well remain statues for a very long time."

That very day the Prince, who had been the Beast, married Beauty. She lived with him in the palace in perfect happiness forever after because, after all, their love was a tale of honest virtue.

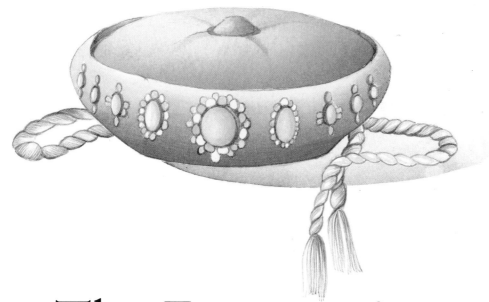

The Emperor's New Clothes

Many years ago there was a grand emperor who was so fond of new clothes that he spent all his money on them. Every hour of the day he changed his clothes.

Whether he was inspecting his soldiers, going to the theater or taking a walk, the real reason he went was to show off his new clothes.

The capital was a very lively city thanks to the many tourists who visited it. One day two thieves arrived who, knowing of the emperor's fondness for clothes, spread the story that they were

weavers and that they knew how to weave the most magnificent cloth in the world. Not only were the colors and the patterns outstandingly beautiful, but the clothes made from this cloth were magic. They were invisible to every person who did not do his job properly or to anyone who was stupid.

"Such clothes are beyond price," thought the emperor. "If I had a suit of this cloth I would know which men in my government are not fit for their jobs, and I would be able to pick out the wise men from the fools. Yes, I certainly must have this cloth."

He gave the thieves a large sum of money and asked them to start their work immediately.

They set up two looms and acted as if they were weaving, although there was nothing at all to be seen. They constantly asked for the finest silk yarn and gold thread; but really they hid everything in their own bags and just pretended to work, long into the night, on the empty looms.

"I would like to know how far they have got with my cloth," thought the emperor a few days later. But he was a bit afraid to go himself when he remembered that anyone who was stupid or no

good at their job could not see the cloth. Although he was sure he had nothing to fear, he decided it would be better to send someone else to check the cloth before he did.

"I will send my faithful old minister to the weavers," decided the emperor. "He is the best person to examine the cloth; he is an intelligent man and knows his job very well."

And so the honest old minister went into the room where the two rogues were working at their empty looms.

"Oh, good heavens!" he thought when he looked, and he opened his eyes wide. "I cannot see a thing."

But the minister did not say anything.

The two weavers beckoned him closer and asked him what he thought of the design and the colors, pointing at their looms. The old man stared at them closely, but he could not see anything for the simple reason that there was nothing to see!

"Oh dear!" he thought. "Am I really that stupid? Am I really unfit for my job? This must never be found out. I don't dare to admit that I cannot see the cloth."

"It is beautiful, it is quite charming!" said the minister aloud, while he put on his glasses. "That design and those colors... yes, I will tell the emperor that I am very pleased."

"We are delighted to hear you say so," said the two weavers, chuckling heartily.

The swindlers then asked for more money, silk yarn and gold thread; they needed a lot for this cloth, they said. But again they put everything in their own pockets; the looms remained empty and they kept on pretending to work.

Soon afterwards, the emperor sent another honest courtier to examine the cloth. The same thing happened to him as to the minister; he stared and stared for a long time, but did not see anything.

"Isn't the cloth lovely?" asked the two thieves while they stroked and exclaimed over the superb design and the beautiful colors that did not exist.

"I am certainly not stupid!" thought the man. "So does this mean that I am not good enough at my job? This is very tricky. I will have to be very

careful if I am not to be found out."

So he praised the cloth and assured them how delighted he was with their choice of colors and patterns.

"No cloth this beautiful has ever been made before," he told the emperor, and the story of the magnificent cloth was on everyone's lips.

At last the emperor decided to go and see the cloth for himself while it was still on the loom. Accompanied by a large number of chosen men, amongst whom were the two men he had sent before, the emperor paid a visit to the two cunning thieves who were still at their looms, busily pretending to weave with nothing.

"Isn't this magnificent?" said the two men who had already seen the work. "The design and the colors suit you perfectly, Your Majesty." And they pointed at the empty loom.

"What is this?" thought the emperor. "I don't see anything! This is terrible! Am I a fool? Am I not capable of governing? This is the worst thing that could have happened to me."

Then suddenly he said aloud, "It is magnificent! I am extremely pleased with it. Please make it into a suit of clothes for me."

He nodded in satisfaction while he looked at the loom. He did not dare to tell the truth. All the people he had taken with him stared hard as well, one after the other. Although they could not see anything, they repeated after the emperor, "It is magnificent! It is charming! It is delightful!"

Everyone appeared happy with the result and the emperor commanded that there was to be a procession the next day, at which he would wear his new suit.

Then the two crooks were given knighthoods and received the title of Gentlemen Weavers.

That night they sat up working in the light of sixteen candles. They pretended to take the cloth from the loom; they cut into the air with a huge pair of scissors and sewed with a needle that had no thread in it. Finally they declared with a great flourish that the suit was finished.

Together with his courtiers, the emperor went to see the finished clothes.

The two thieves both stood with their arms in the air as if they were holding up something, and said, "Here are the trousers, Your Majesty. Here is the jacket, here is the cloak. They are as light as a feather, so light that it may seem as if you are not

wearing anything, but that is one of the important qualities of this cloth."

"Yes, of course," answered the courtiers.

But they did not see anything; after all, there was nothing to see!

"Would Your Highness be graciously pleased to take off your clothes?" asked the thieves. "Then you can try on the new ones in front of the big mirror."

The emperor took his clothes off and the thieves pretended to dress him. He turned round and round in front of the mirror.

"Good gracious! How well it suits His Majesty! What a perfect fit!" exclaimed all the courtiers. "What style! What colours! What a wonderful suit!"

Then the chief master of ceremonies entered.

"The canopy which is to be carried over Your Majesty in the procession is waiting outside," he said.

"Excellent! I am ready," answered the emperor. "I think I look quite good in these clothes."

And he twirled in front of the mirror one more time to look at the splendid suit.

The attendants, who had to carry the cloak's long train, pretended to pick it up from the ground; then they held their hands as if they were holding the train because they did not want anyone to think that they could not see it.

The emperor walked very proudly in the procession under his beautiful canopy, and all the people in the street and at the windows cried, "What a splendid costume! How gracious the train is! What a perfect fit!"

Nobody would let anyone else think that he could not see anything. Never had the emperor's clothes been so admired before.

Then a little child pushed to the front of the crowd. "But he's not wearing anything!" he cried.

"Heavens, listen to the voice of innocence!" said the child's father.

But soon afterwards all the people started to whisper and repeat the child's words.

"There is a little child who says the emperor isn't wearing any clothes at all!" whispered the crowd.

"Indeed, there are no clothes at all!" everyone exclaimed at last.

The emperor then felt extremely foolish for he realized that they were quite right. However, he held his head up high and continued until the end of the procession.

The attendants continued respectfully carrying the train that did not exist, until at last they were once again safely inside the palace.

And do you know? The emperor was never quite so vain about his clothes after that!

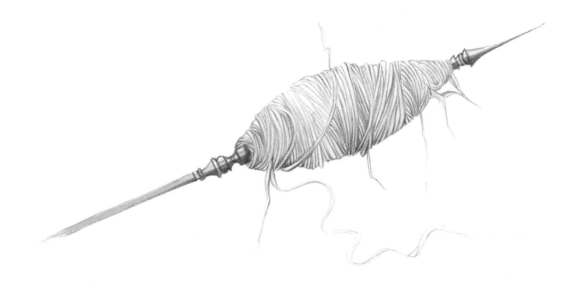

Rumpelstiltskin

Once upon a time there was a miller who was very poor, but he had a beautiful daughter. One day it happened that he had the chance to speak to the king, and in order to seem important to him he said, "I have a daughter who can spin gold out of straw."

"Now that is a talent which interests me," answered the king. "If your daughter is as clever as you say, bring her to my castle tomorrow and I will put her to the test."

When the young girl arrived, he took her to a

room full of straw, gave her a reel and a spinning wheel and said, "Now you will start working, and if between now and tomorrow morning you have not spun this straw into gold, you will die."

Thereupon he locked the door securely and she was left all alone.

There sat the poor miller's daughter, not knowing what to do. She had no idea how to spin straw into gold and she became so frightened that she started to cry.

Suddenly the door opened and a little man entered who said to her, "Good evening, beautiful miller's daughter. Why are you crying?"

"Alas!" answered the young girl. "I have to spin all this straw into gold and I don't know how."

"What will you give me if I spin it for you?" asked the little man.

"My necklace," answered the girl.

The little man took the necklace, sat down behind the spinning wheel and started to spin, spin, spin. He only spun three times and the reel was full. He replaced it by another one and started to spin, spin, spin; he only spun three times and the second one was full too! He did this all night until dawn broke.

So all the straw was spun and all the reels were full of gold.

As soon as the sun rose the king arrived. When he saw all the gold he was extremely pleased. But he was a greedy man and wanted more.

He took the miller's daughter to another room full of straw, which was even larger than the one before, and ordered her to spin all that straw into gold in one night if she wanted to stay alive.

When she was left alone the young girl started to cry.

Then the door opened once again. The little man appeared and said, "What will you give me if I spin this straw into gold?"

"The ring that I wear on my finger," answered the young girl.

The little man took the ring, sat himself down behind the spinning wheel, and by the next morning he had spun all the straw into sparkling gold.

The king was delighted at the sight of all this gold, but he still wasn't satisfied. He took the miller's daughter to another room full of straw, even larger than the first two, and commanded, "You will spin all this straw for me tonight, and if you succeed you will become my wife."

"Although she is only a miller's daughter," he thought, "I couldn't find a richer wife!"

When the young girl was alone, the little man arrived again and said, "What will you give me this time if I spin the straw into gold?"

"I don't have anything more to give," answered the young girl.

"Well, promise me your first child if you become queen," said the little man.

"That's never likely to happen!" thought the miller's daughter.

Still, she promised the little man his wish and again he spun all the straw into gold.

When the king arrived the next morning and saw all the gold he prepared the wedding and the pretty miller's daughter became queen, much to her surprise.

One year later, when she had forgotten all about the little man, she gave birth to a beautiful child.

Then one day he suddenly walked into her room and said, "Well, give me what you have promised."

The queen was terrified and offered the little man all the treasures of the kingdom not to take her child.

But the little man answered, "No, I have no need of treasure. You must keep your promise."

Then the queen started to moan and weep. The little man felt sorry for her, and he said, "I will give you three days. If within that time you discover my name, I will let you keep your child."

Throughout the whole night the queen thought about all the names she had ever heard, and she sent a messenger through the country to find out every name that existed.

When the little man arrived the next day she

started with Caspar, Melchior, Balthazar, and said one name after another until she knew no more.

Every time the little man said, "That is not my name."

The next day she had inquiries made throughout the entire neighborhood for the name of every single person, and she repeated the strangest and the rarest names to the little man.

"Isn't your name Cowribs, or Leg-of-Mutton, or Spiderlegs?" she said.

But still he answered, "That is not my name."

The third day the messenger came back and said he was not able to find any new names.

"However," he said, "when I arrived at a huge mountain at the corner of a forest where the foxes and the hares say goodnight to each other, I saw a fire burning in front of a little house. A very strange little man was dancing around this fire. He was hopping on one leg and singing:

"Today I bake. Tomorrow I brew beer.
The day after tomorrow I will bring the
queen's child here.
How lucky I am that nobody knows
That Rumpelstiltskin is my name."

You can imagine how delighted the queen was when she heard that!

Soon afterwards, the little man entered and asked her, "What is my name?"

She answered, "Is your name Harry?"

"No."

"Is your name Bert?"

"No."

Then the queen laughed and said, "Is your name, by any chance … Rumpelstiltskin?"

"It must have been the devil who told you that! It must have been the devil who told you that!" screamed the little man.

And in his rage he stamped his right foot so violently on the floor that he disappeared through the ground and was never seen again!

Florinda and Yoringal

Once upon a time there was an old castle in the middle of a huge, dark forest where an old woman lived all alone. She was a witch; during the day she changed herself into a cat or an owl, and at night she turned back to a human being.

She used magic to entice rabbits and birds to come to her. Then she would boil or roast them for her dinner.

A powerful spell surrounded the castle. If a man approached within a hundred steps he would find

himself powerless to move. There he would be forced to stay, like a statue, until the witch decided to free him. But if a young girl approached, the witch would change her into a bird and lock her up in a cage. She had seven thousand cages in her castle, each containing rare birds.

Near to the forest lived a girl named Florinda. She was the most beautiful girl in the world and she was engaged to a handsome young man named Yoringal. They loved each other very much and were to be married soon.

One day they went for a walk in the forest so that they could spend some time alone.

"We must be careful not to go too close to the castle," warned Yoringal as they set off.

Late that afternoon a change seemed to fall on the forest. The sun still shone between the thick, green trees, but the turtle doves who lived there began to sing a sad song which made Florinda cry.

Then both Florinda and Yoringal began to moan. They felt miserable, as if they were about to die, and it wasn't long before they realized that they had lost their way.

It was almost sunset. Yoringal looked through the bushes and saw that they were very close to

the castle walls. He trembled at the sight.

Then he heard Florinda singing:

"Little bird with your red ring
Singing sorrow! Sorrow! Sorrow!
Singing the dove's death,
Singing sorrow… Chirp! Chirp! Chirp!"

Before his very eyes, Florinda changed into a nightingale! Then an owl with haunting eyes appeared and flew three times around her crying, "Who-oo! Who-oo! Who-oo!"

Yoringal found that he could not move an inch. He stood like a stone, unable to cry, speak or move his hands and feet.

Then the sun set. The owl flew into a bush and from its dark leaves appeared an old hunch-backed woman, sallow-skinned and scraggy, with big red eyes and a long, crooked nose. She mumbled something, took the nightingale in her hand and carried it away. Yoringal was helpless.

At first the young man despaired that he would be a statue for ever, but after a while the witch returned and began to chant in a sinister voice, "Oh Zachiel! When the moon shines on the cage, break the spell at the right time, Zachiel."

Then Yoringal was free. He fell on his knees before the old witch and begged her to give him back his Florinda. She told him he would never see Florinda again, then disappeared.

"What is to become of me?" sighed Yoringal.

He wandered all night until he came to a village he'd never been to before. There he worked as a shepherd for many years. He often walked near to the castle, careful not to get too close!

Then one night he dreamt he found a red flower in the middle of which was a beautiful, big pearl. In his dream he picked the flower and took it to the castle. Everything he touched with that flower was freed from the witch's evil spell, including Florinda.

When he awoke next morning, Yoringal began to search high and low for such a flower. He searched for nine days, and early on the ninth day he found it. In the middle was a big dewdrop, as shiny as the finest pearl.

Carefully he retraced his steps and returned to the castle.

This time the standing spell didn't effect him and he was able to walk right up to the door. Yoringal was delighted. He touched the door with

the flower and it opened. He entered, crossed the courtyard, then stopped and listened. There was such a twittering and cheeping coming from the tower that it wasn't difficult for him to guess where the seven thousand birds were imprisoned!

When the witch saw Yoringal she fell into a great rage. She cursed and spat poison at him, but she could not get nearer to him than two steps. He ignored her and hurried towards the bird cages.

But, alas, how could he find his beloved Florinda amongst the hundreds of nightingales?

In the corner of his eye, Yoringal noticed that the witch had stolen a cage and was trying to escape through the door. He leapt towards her and touched the cage with his flower. The witch immediately lost all her powers and Florinda stood there, as beautiful as ever!

With a cry of joy she flung her arms around his neck. Then together they changed all the other birds back to young girls again and returned home, where they lived happily ever after.

Cinderella

Once upon a time there was a man whose first wife died and who married for the second time the haughtiest and proudest woman in the world. She had two daughters who took after her in every way.

The man had a young daughter from his first marriage, but she was a sweet and kind girl. She took after her mother, who had been the nicest person in the world.

The man's new wife could not stand this young girl's good qualities which made her daughters

seem even more detestable. She ordered her to do the dirtiest work around the house: she was the one who did the dishes, cleaned the stairs, and polished all the rooms.

She was made to sleep in the attic on a very hard mattress, while the two sisters had rooms with polished floors, where they slept in soft beds and had mirrors in which they could see themselves from head to toe.

The poor girl suffered in silence and did not dare to complain to her father. When the housework was done she would go to the fireplace and sit in the ashes.

The spiteful sisters thought this was very funny and gave her the name of Cinderella. But although the poor girl had to wear old-fashioned, ragged, cast-off clothes, she was still a hundred times more beautiful than the two sisters, even in their most magnificent dresses.

Now it happened that the king's son organized a ball and sent out invitations to all the important people of the country. When the two sisters received their invitation they were delighted and spent all their time choosing the clothes and the hairstyles that they would wear to the ball.

This caused a great deal of extra work for Cinderella because she was the one who had to iron the clothes and starch the lace collars.

The only thing they could talk about was the way they would be dressed.

"I will wear my red velvet dress with lace trimming," said one.

"I will wear my cloak embroidered with golden flowers and my diamond brooch," said her sister.

Of course, Cinderella was called to help. She gave them the best advice she could and even offered to do their hair.

They said to her, "Cinderella, wouldn't you like to go to the ball? With your raggedy clothes and dirty face – what a sight you'd be!"

Cinderella blushed, for inside she really did want to go to the ball. "Sisters, you are laughing at me, that makes it even worse," she said.

"You are right, everyone would have a good laugh if they saw Cinderella at the ball," sneered the pair.

Then Cinderella had an idea.

"Maybe I could go to the ball," she said. "Won't you please lend me the yellow dress that you wear around the house so I can go with you?"

"Really, I don't think so!" exclaimed the elder sister. "Lend my dress to such a grubby little Cinders? You must think I am stupid!"

And so the matter was closed. You couldn't have blamed Cinderella if she had completely ruined the sisters' hair, but she was a kind girl and arranged it beautifully, although they did not thank her for it.

The sisters were so excited that they could not eat for two days before the ball. They broke more than a dozen corset-laces because they pulled them in so tightly in order to make themselves look

slender, and they were constantly primping in front of the mirror.

At last the great day arrived. Poor Cinderella waved goodbye to the sisters, then she sat down at the fireplace and began to weep.

Her godmother, who saw her bitter tears, asked her what was wrong.

"I want to… I want to…" Cinderella was crying so hard that she could not get the words out.

But her godmother, who was also a fairy, said, "You would like to go to the ball, wouldn't you?"

"Yes," sighed Cinderella.

"Well, if you are a good girl, I will send you there," said her fairy godmother.

She began to give Cinderella the most peculiar instructions. "Go into the garden and bring me a pumpkin," she said.

Cinderella went and picked the most beautiful pumpkin she could find. She took it indoors to her fairy godmother, although she was wondering how a pumpkin was going to help her get to the ball.

Her fairy godmother hollowed it out until there was nothing left but the shell, tapped it with her magic wand – and the pumpkin changed into a beautiful golden carriage!

Then the fairy godmother looked in the mouse-trap where she found six live mice. She told Cinderella to lift up the lid of the trap and to let the mice out one by one.

As the mice crept out, she tapped them with her magic wand which changed them into beautiful horses to draw the carriage. Then she wondered what could serve as a coachman.

"I will see if there is a rat in the rat-trap," said Cinderella. "A rat would make a good coachman."

Cinderella fetched the rat-trap which had three

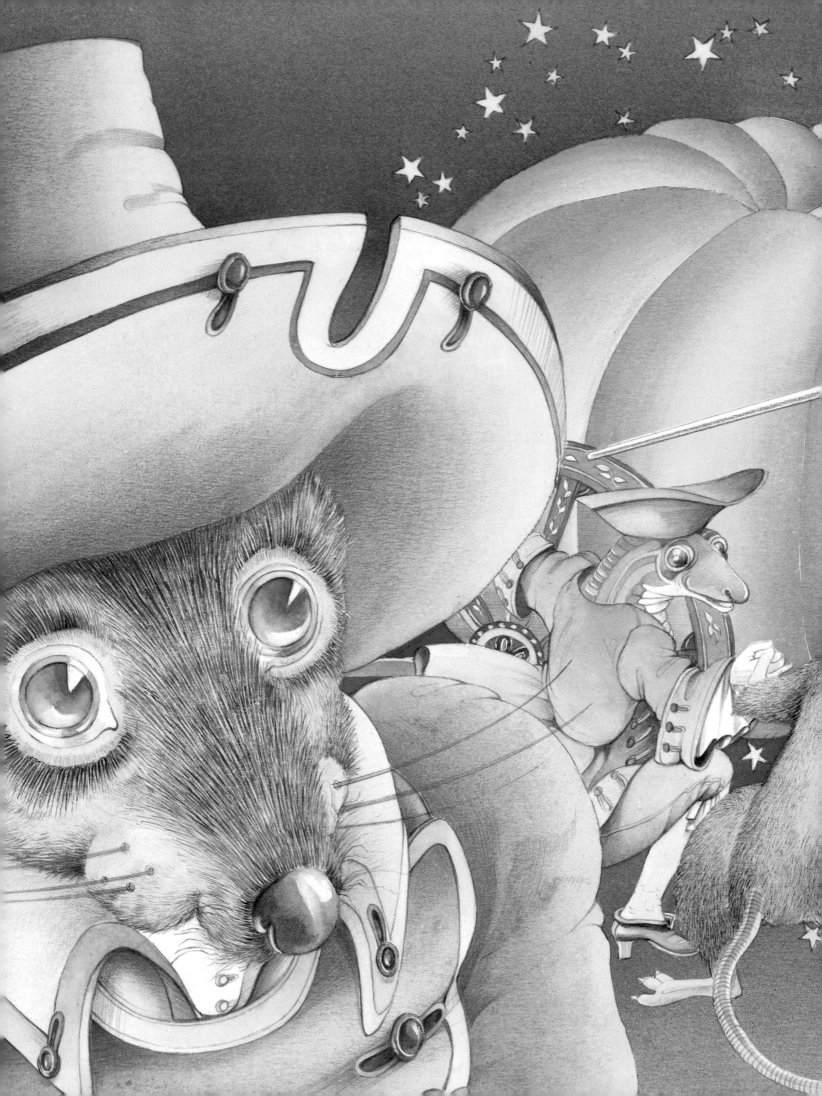

fat rats in it. The fairy godmother chose the one with the finest whiskers. When she touched it with her magic wand, it changed into a coachman with the most handsome moustache in the world!

Then she said to Cinderella, "Go and look behind the watering-can. You will find six lizards there. Bring them to me."

Cinderella had no sooner brought them to her fairy godmother than she changed them into footmen. They stepped up behind the carriage with their brightly-patterned uniforms and hung on as if they had never done anything else in their lives.

Then the fairy godmother said, "Well, now you can go to the ball in style. Aren't you delighted?"

"Yes, but how can I possibly go to the ball in these wretched clothes?" replied the girl.

Just one touch of the magic wand changed Cinderella's rags into a dress of gold and silver material, embroidered with precious stones. Finally the fairy godmother gave her a pair of glass slippers.

All dressed up, Cinderella got into the carriage. Her fairy godmother warned her to be home by midnight for the spell would break at the twelfth chime of the clock.

The girl promised her fairy godmother that she would and drove off.

The king's son had been told that an unknown princess was about to arrive at the ball, so he ran outside to welcome her. He helped Cinderella down from the carriage and led her into the ballroom.

As soon as everyone saw her they were awestruck. The dancing ceased and the fiddlers stopped playing as they all admired her perfect beauty.

Even the king himself, although he was an old man, could not keep his eyes off her, and he whispered to the queen that he had not seen such a beautiful young lady for a long time. The queen agreed with him, for truly the beautiful stranger outshone every other person in the room.

All the women studied her hairstyle and dress closely, wondering what far-off country could produce such elegant gowns in such magnificent materials. They were determined to remember every last detail so that they would be able to copy them next time there was a grand occasion.

The prince seated Cinderella in the best place and paid her many compliments. Then, later he led her on to the dance floor. She danced so gracefully that everyone admired her even more.

After the first round of dances there was a fine banquet, but the prince could not eat anything because he was too absorbed with the lovely stranger.

Cinderella sat next to the sisters and gave them all her attention, offering them oranges and lemons which the prince had given her. They were extremely surprised, but they did not recognize her at all.

Then the dancing started again. All the young men wanted to dance with the lovely girl, but the prince didn't give anyone a chance. Cinderella danced every dance with the prince, and when they rested he stayed at her side, making sure that she wanted for nothing.

Cinderella had never been happier in her life. Indeed, she was so absorbed with the handsome young man and his attention that she quite forgot her fairy godmother's warning.

Then the palace clock began to chime.

At the first stroke of midnight Cinderella realized her mistake and sprang to her feet, fleeing the ballroom.

The prince followed, but he could not catch her. However, in her hurry she dropped one of her dainty glass slippers. Still, the young girl ran and ran, not stopping to pick it up or even to look behind her.

Cinderella arrived home exhausted, without a carriage or her footmen, and dressed in her old clothes. Nothing remained of her splendor but the other glass slipper.

The prince asked the guards at the palace door if they had seen the princess leave. They said they

had not seen anyone go out but a young girl dressed in rags, who looked more like a farmer's daughter than a lady.

When the sisters came home a little later on, Cinderella asked them if they'd enjoyed the ball. Excitedly they told her about the beautiful stranger who'd captivated the prince, and how she had run off suddenly into the night, leaving one slipper on the palace steps.

They told her that the prince had picked up the fallen glass slipper and had gazed at it for the rest

of the evening. He had definitely fallen head over heels in love with the beautiful stranger, even though he didn't know who she was.

The sisters were telling the truth, for a few days later the king's son publicly announced that he would marry the girl whose foot would fit perfectly into the slipper.

But although all the princesses, then all the duchesses, and then all the rest of the court ladies in the land tried it on, not one could fit the delicate shoe.

The slipper was eventually brought to the two sisters, who squeezed and pushed, and pushed and squeezed, and tried with all their might to fit a foot into it, but all in vain.

Then Cinderella smiled and said, "I would like to try the slipper and see if it fits me!"

The sisters laughed and made fun of her, but the courtier had been given orders to let all the girls in the land try on the slipper. So he sat Cinderella down and, to everyone's surprise, the slipper fitted perfectly!

The two sisters were astonished, but not half as astonished as they were when Cinderella took the other glass slipper from her pocket and put it on.

At this moment the fairy godmother appeared and tapped Cinderella's clothes with her magic wand. At once the rags changed into a dress even more beautiful than the ones she had worn before.

Then the sisters recognized her as the kind lady they had met at the ball. They dropped to their knees and begged her to forgive them for all the suffering they had caused her.

Cinderella embraced them and said that she forgave them with all her heart.

Then she was taken to the prince in her splendid dress. He thought she was more beautiful than ever and, a few day later, he married her.

And, of course, you don't need me to tell you that they then lived happily ever after!

Reynard
and the
Fishermen

It was winter and Reynard the Fox had no more food in his store. Driven by starvation, he roamed near the villages without fearing the inhabitants. He hid under a hedge at the side of the main road, waiting for something exciting to happen.

Soon a little cart came along the road. In it were two fishermen who wanted to do business in the city. They had a huge catch of fresh herrings to sell, for the north wind had been blowing the

whole week and the fish were plentiful.

They also had baskets filled to the brim with fish, large and small, from the lakes and from the rivers: pike, eel, carp, trout and salmon.

Reynard got very excited at the sight and the smell of the fish cart and decided that this was his chance. So he stretched himself out in the middle of the road as if he were dead. He put his feet in the air, closed his eyes and held his breath.

One of the fishermen noticed him and said to his partner, "Let's pick up that fox. That's a good skin, easily gained!"

They approached Reynard cautiously, touched him and then turned him over, certain that he was dead. Then they estimated the value of his skin.

"We will sell it for three silver pieces," said one.

"No, we will easily get four silver pieces for it," said the other. "Maybe more – look how white the throat is!"

They threw Reynard into the back of the cart and continued on their way, talking cheerfully.

Reynard heard them talking and had a good laugh to himself at the bottom of the cart.

He lay flat on his stomach on top of the baskets, and, with his sharp teeth, he nibbled at a juicy

herring. Then he ate thirty more. He crunched the raw fish, bone and all, between his teeth. It didn't bother Reynard that there was no salt, herbs or mustard!

The first basket was soon emptied, then he started on the second one. He picked out half a dozen eels that were strung together through their gills to form a loop. Reynard put his head and throat through the loop.

Then he arranged the eels securely on his back and jumped down from the cart, at the same time shouting to the fishermen, "Goodbye and have a safe trip home! I only took a couple of eels and I gladly leave you the rest!"

The fishermen jumped down to follow him, shaking their fists and hitting their heads.

"How could we have been so stupid! To the devil with this evil beast!" they cried.

But Reynard ran much faster than they could and easily escaped. When they returned to their cart, completely exhausted, all they found were empty baskets.

Rapunzel

Once upon a time there was a man and a woman who had wanted a child for a long time. Then, one day, the woman believed that her wish would be granted at last.

Their house had a little window at the back which looked out over a magnificent garden filled with beautiful flowers and all kinds of wonderful herbs and vegetables. The garden was surrounded by a high wall and no one dared to go in because it belonged to a powerful witch.

One day as the woman stood at the window and looked into the garden she noticed a bed full of splendid radishes which looked so fresh and so delicious that she longed to eat them. The longing to eat those radishes grew stronger day by day, and since this honest woman knew she could never have them, she grew thinner and became pale and weak.

Her husband became worried and asked, "What is the matter, my dear wife?"

"Alas," she said, "if I cannot eat some radishes from the garden behind our house, I will die!"

Her husband, who loved her very much, said, "I will not let you die, wife."

At dusk he climbed over the wall and went into the witch's garden where he hastily picked a handful of radishes and brought them to his wife. Immediately she made a salad out of them and greedily ate it. They tasted so delicious that the next day her desire for more was even greater.

To keep her contented, her husband knew he would have to be brave and go to the garden again. He waited until evening, when it began to get dark, but when he jumped down from the wall, he found himself face to face with the witch.

"How dare you come into my garden to steal my radishes," she said furiously.

"Alas!" he replied, "I did not come here by my own free will, but was forced to because of the danger that is threatening my wife. She saw your radishes from our window and had such a desire for them that she believed she would die if she could not eat them."

Then the witch said, "If everything you have told me is true, I will allow you to take as many radishes as you want. In return you must give me

the child your wife will bear. The child will have a good home and I will be a mother to it."

The man was so terrified that he agreed to everything. When his wife gave birth to a little girl, the witch came to their home and took the baby away with her. She called her Rapunzel.

Rapunzel became the most beautiful little girl under the sun. When she was twelve years old, the witch locked her up in a tower in the middle of the forest. The tower had neither stairs nor doors, only a little window at the top. Every time the witch wanted to go to the top of the tower, she stood underneath and cried out:

"Rapunzel, Rapunzel,
Let down your hair!"

Rapunzel had wonderful long hair, as fine as spun gold. Whenever she heard the witch calling she unpinned her hair, fastened it around one of the window hooks and let it fall to the ground. Then the witch climbed up the golden rope.

It so happened that the king's son was riding through the forest one day. As he passed nearby the tower, he heard such a glorious sound that he drew up his horse to listen.

The beautiful sound was Rapunzel, trying to pass the time by singing. In vain, the prince looked for a door into the tower. However, the song had touched his heart so much that he returned to the forest every single day to listen to it.

One day he saw the witch come to the foot of the tower. The prince hid behind a tree to watch and heard her say:

"Rapunzel, Rapunzel,
Let down your hair."

Rapunzel then let down her long braids and the witch climbed up.

"So that is the way into the tower," he said to himself. "Well, I will just have to try my luck."

The next day at dusk, he went to the tower and called up:

"Rapunzel, Rapunzel,
Let down your hair."

Rapunzel's hair tumbled down immediately and the prince climbed up.

At first Rapunzel was terrified to see a strange man, but the prince told her gently that he had

heard her sing and that his heart had been touched
by her song.

Rapunzel then forgot her fears and the prince
asked if she would have him for her husband.

She saw that he was young and handsome, and
thought, "He loves me more than the old witch
does." So she agreed, and gave him her hand.

The prince came to visit her every evening and
the witch, who only came during the day, knew
nothing at all about it.

Then, one day Rapunzel said without thinking, "Tell me, how is it that you are slow and heavy and pull my hair, whereas the prince climbs up to me so quickly?"

"You wicked child," cried the witch. "What is this I hear? So you have deceived me!"

In her rage she took Rapunzel's beautiful hair, wound it a couple of times around her hand and, snip! snap! she quickly cut it off. All the golden hair and the marvelous braids fell on the floor.

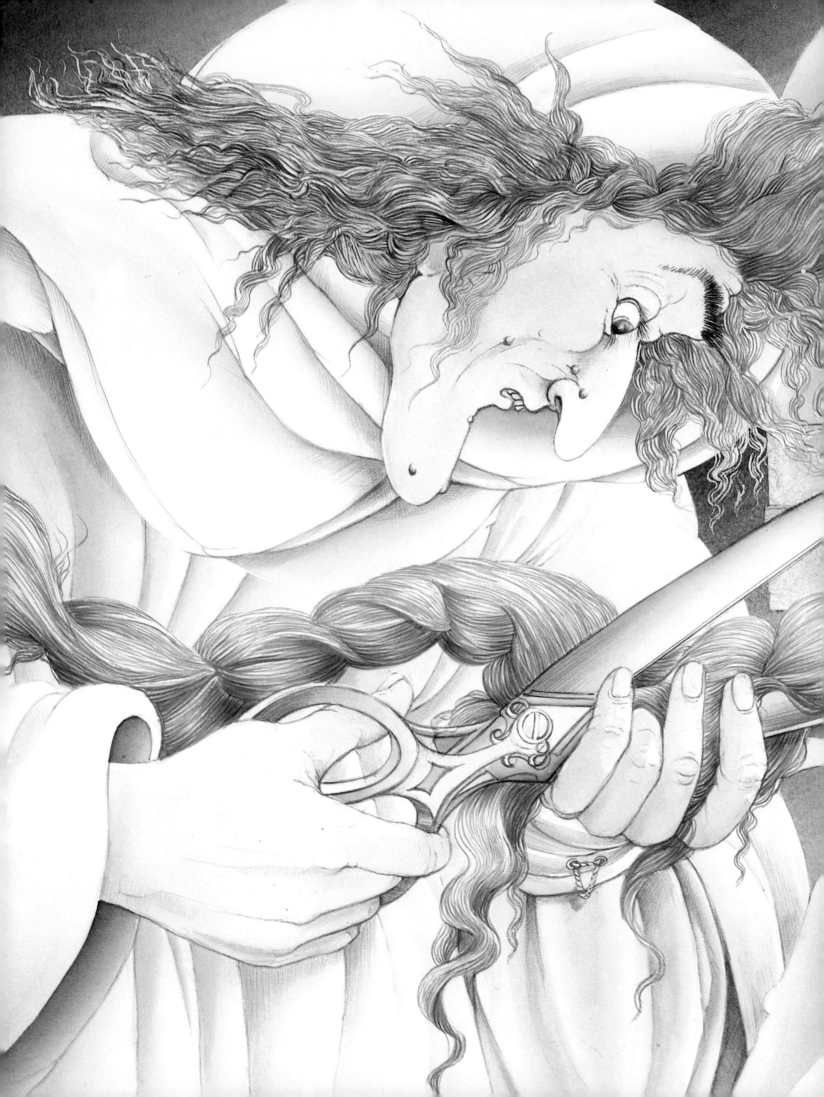

Then the witch took Rapunzel to a very remote place and abandoned her to live in loneliness.

That evening, as dusk fell, the witch hid herself in the tower. Soon the king's son arrived and called:

"Rapunzel, Rapunzel,
Let down your hair!"

When the witch heard this she fastened poor Rapunzel's hair to the window hook and let it fall to the ground. When the prince climbed up to the window he found this wicked witch instead of his sweet Rapunzel.

She looked at him with haunting, evil eyes and said, "Rapunzel is lost to you forever. You will never see her again!"

The prince was devastated. In his misery he fell from the window and landed in a bramble bush. He was not killed, but the thorns on the bush made him blind.

Unable to think of life without Rapunzel, the young man wandered into the forest. He lived on berries and roots, and drifted in this way for many years, until one day he arrived by chance at the lonely place where Rapunzel lived in misery.

All at once he heard a voice that was familiar to him and walked towards the sound. When he was close, Rapunzel recognized him. She was over-joyed to see him, but sad when she noticed his sightless eyes. She put her arms around his neck and wept.

Two tears fell from her eyes into the eyes of the blind prince. Instantly they became clear again and he could see as he did before. Then, happily reunited with his love, he carried Rapunzel to his kingdom where they married and lived happily ever after.

Ali Baba
and the Forty Thieves

Once upon a time, in a Persian city, there lived two brothers who loved each other very much and often visited each other. One was a merchant called Cassim and the other was a woodcutter called Ali Baba.

One day, on his way to the forest with his three donkeys, Ali Baba saw a cloud of dust in the distance. It was undoubtedly a large and possibly unfriendly group of horsemen because very few people passed along this road. Since he was afraid of being robbed, Ali Baba looked for a hiding place.

Not far away was a very high rock, next to  which stood a tall tree. Ali Baba hid his donkeys, climbed into the tree and waited.

The cloud of dust quickly became bigger and soon the group arrived. There were forty men, each carrying a big bag on his shoulders. The men jumped down from their horses and tied them next to the rock.

Then the leader approached the rock and cried, "Open, Sesame!"

To Ali Baba's astonishment, a door opened in the rock face. The men disappeared into the cave and the door closed behind them. Ali Baba stayed in his tree, not daring to climb down right away.

While he was thinking what to do next, the door opened again. The men came out and the leader commanded the door, "Close, Sesame!"

It rumbled shut. Then the men mounted their horses again and rode off.

When they were far away, Ali Baba climbed down from the tree, stood in front of the rock and, after hesitating for a time, he also cried, "Open, Sesame!"

Once again the rock face opened and Ali Baba

walked into a most amazing cave. There was enough light inside to see a collection of fabulous treasures – silk material, rich fabrics, carpets and, above all, bags overflowing with gold and silver. It was obviously the secret hide-out of a group of robbers.

After Ali Baba had recovered from his astonishment, he gathered as much gold as his three donkeys could carry and closed the cave with the magic words.

When he arrived home, he emptied his bags in front of his wife, who was dazzled by the gold. He then told her all about his adventure.

"We are rich!" she cried, dancing and clapping her hands. "But how much exactly do we have?"

"Enough to live in peace for the rest of our days," answered Ali Baba.

"I want to be sure. We must count it!" his wife demanded.

Ali Baba did not see any reason for this, but he did not want to upset his wife so he let her have her way. She immediately went to Cassim to ask him for a measuring cup.

Cassim's wife opened the door.

"A measuring cup?" she asked, astonished.

"Yes, the biggest one you have!" replied Ali Baba's wife.

Cassim's wife lent her the cup, but she secretly stuck some candle-wax on the bottom because she wanted to know what there was to measure at a poor woodcutter's house.

When Ali Baba's wife returned home she began to scoop up the gold with the cup. She filled it

once, twice, many times. A little while later she returned the cup to her sister-in-law but, in her hurry, she did not notice that there was a gold piece stuck to the bottom.

When Cassim came home his wife said, "Sit down here! I have something to tell you."

"What is it?" asked Cassim.

"Cassim, do you think you are rich?" she said.

"Enough to be happy," he replied.

"Well, Ali Baba is a thousand times richer than you are," said his wife. "He has so much gold at home that he needs a measuring cup to count it!"

And she showed him the gold piece.

Cassim, who was a bit jealous, went to his brother's house and said, "Tell me, I beg you, how do you have so much gold at your house?"

Ali Baba realized his secret had been discovered and because he loved his brother he told him everything, including the magic words to open the door to the thieves' hide-out.

Cassim thanked him. Early the next morning, he set off with ten mules to find the rock.

"Open, Sesame!" he cried when he reached it.

The door opened. He went inside and the door closed behind him.

For a moment he was astonished by all the glittering treasure, then he pulled himself together and began to fill the bags. When they were full he tried to leave the cave, but he couldn't remember the magic words.

"Open, Ogre!" he tried.

The door stayed closed. He tried again and again. No matter what words he said, he could not think of the right one, so hours later he was still locked in.

As ill luck would have it, the thieves arrived at the cave. When they opened the magic door Cassim took the chance to escape. He was caught immediately by the thieves who killed him on the spot and cut him up into four pieces.

The next day Ali Baba came to the rock in search of his brother. To his horror he discovered his brother's remains. Weeping with shock and grief, he put the four pieces that were left of his brother on the donkeys and returned home to Cassim's widow to tell her the dreadful news.

Now, Cassim had a very clever servant whose name was Morgiane.

"Morgiane, we will have to cover up the true reason for Cassim's death!" said Ali Baba.

"Don't worry, I know how to handle that!" she replied.

The next day the servant went several times to the chemist, pretending that her master had fallen ill. Each time she asked for stronger and stronger medicines, saying that he was going from bad to worse. The following day, no one was surprised, therefore, to hear that Cassim had died.

Also in the city lived a very old, wise garment-maker called Baba Moustafa. Morgiane asked him

to come to her in secret, bringing the tools of his trade. Baba Moustafa, who was suspicious, did not agree to do so unless he was given a large sum of money. He was then blindfolded and led into Cassim's room.

There Morgiane took off the blindfold and asked him to sew her poor master's body back together. Baba Moustafa did so and, after he was finished, he was blindfolded again and taken home. In this way Cassim had a dignified funeral and no one was the least suspicious.

Ali Baba inherited his brother's house. As he liked that house better than his own, he moved in with his wife and they lived together with Cassim's widow and Morgiane the servant.

In the meantime, the forty thieves had not forgotten the intruder in their cave.

"Someone else knows our secret!" said the leader. "The pile of gold is smaller. Who will go into the city to see what can be found out?"

One of the thieves volunteered and left early the next morning in disguise. He soon found Baba Moustafa's shop in which the old wise man was busy with his work.

"Good man!" the thief said to the old man.

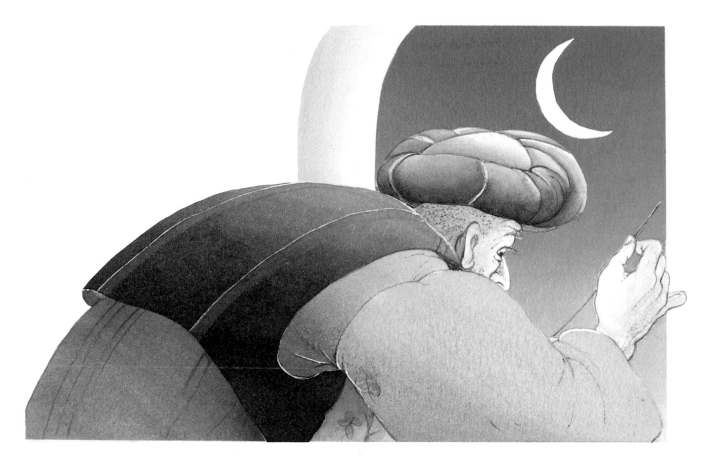

"How can you still see so clearly at your age?"

"Eh? I can see that you are not from around here!" said Baba Moustafa. "My eyes are the best in the city. Why, not long ago I sewed a dead man back together in a room much darker than this!"

"Go on... Where was that?" asked the thief.

"I don't know. I was taken there blindfolded," replied Baba Moustafa.

The thief held out a couple of gold pieces. "Take me there!"

"I told you, I was blindfolded!" said Baba Moustafa.

"Try to remember in which direction you were led!" pressed the thief.

Baba Moustafa accepted the challenge and, as he had a good memory, they soon arrived in front of Cassim's house, which was now Ali Baba's.

The thief thanked Baba Moustafa, then he secretly made a cross with chalk on the door and went back into the forest.

Shortly afterwards, Morgiane discovered the mark. She assumed that this mark was not a good sign so she took a piece of chalk of the same colour and drew crosses on all the other doors in the neighborhood.

That same night, the forty thieves sneaked into the city. They looked for the door marked with a cross, intending to kill the people who lived there. But when they found that every door had a cross they left in great anger.

The following day the leader decided to take things into his own hands. He too found Baba Moustafa, who led him to Ali Baba's house. The leader examined it closely and very soon he had an idea.

When he got back to the forest he sent his men to buy some mules and forty leather oil jars.

When everything had been bought the leader filled one of the jars with oil, leaving the others empty. Then he ordered all his men into the empty jars which he then sealed, leaving just a little airhole in each lid.

That night he drove his strange convoy into the city. Ali Baba was enjoying the cool, night air when the leader of the thieves stopped outside, pretending that he was an oil merchant bound for

market the following day. He said that he had come a long distance and was very tired.

Ali Baba did not recognize him at all.

"You are welcome here," Ali Baba said. "Come into my house and spend the night!"

The fake merchant put his jars in the courtyard under the window of the room where he would be staying. While Ali Baba was out of earshot the leader went to each jar and gave his orders.

"Can you hear me? When I throw little stones out of my window, split the vases from top to bottom with your knives and get out! I will then tell you what to do."

He went to bed early, keeping all his clothes on, ready for action.

Meanwhile, Morgiane was working in the kitchen when her oil lamp suddenly went out.

"Oh! What a time to run out of oil!" she cried.

"Well, go into the courtyard," said Abdalla, another servant. "There is plenty of oil as long as the merchant is here!"

So Morgiane took a jug and went outside. When she approached the first jar, she heard, "Hey! Is it time?"

That voice certainly came from the jar!

Morgiane, who was a quick thinker, realized the danger immediately and answered in a whisper, "Not yet, but soon!"

She went to the other jars, hearing the same question and giving the same answer, until she found the oil jar.

First she lit her lamp again, then she poured the oil from the last jar into a large copper pan which she put on the stove until it boiled. Then she poured boiling oil into each jar, killing all the thieves quickly and quietly.

Later, when the leader of the thieves threw the little stones out of his window, he was angry that there was no response. He went outside to wake up the thieves, but when he smelled the hot oil and leather he thought it wiser to leave quickly!

Next morning, when Ali Baba came back from the bath house, he was surprised to see the jars still in his courtyard.

Morgiane told him to open one of them and when he saw what was in it he jumped back in fright. Then the servant told him about how she had rescued him and his family.

Ali Baba realized that the men in the jars must be the thieves from the cave with the magic door.

As a reward he gave Morgiane her freedom.

He buried the bodies, sold the mules and carefully hid the weapons and the leather jars.

However, although the leader of the thieves had run off, he was not that far away. He longed to take his revenge on the man who had invaded his hoard and destroyed his gang.

In a little while he returned to the city, rented a shop and became a cloth merchant, calling himself Cogia Houssain. He made it his business to become very friendly with Ali Baba's son. He was extremely courteous to the young man, and finally succeeded in being invited to his father's house.

Ali Baba invited his son's new friend to stay for dinner, but the man refused.

"Why do you refuse?" said Ali Baba, surprised.

"It is because I can only eat food without salt, and this creates too much trouble for the people who invite me," said the phoney merchant.

"That makes no difference to me!" cried Ali Baba. "I can offer you a meal without salt. Come on! I beg you! Do me the honor and stay."

The man then accepted. Morgiane was annoyed that she had to start all over again, preparing food without salt, but she did as she was asked.

227

She thought the guest must be a very strange man to make such demands. Under the pretext of helping Abdalla, she served at the table so that she could have a look at the stranger.

Morgiane was more perceptive than Ali Baba. She recognized the cruel leader of the thieves straight away, even though he was disguised as a cloth merchant. She saw the knife he was hiding under his clothes and devised a very bold plan.

When they had eaten their dessert, she dressed herself up as a dancer, with a sword fixed to her belt as if it was part of the costume. Abdalla accompanied her playing the tambourine. As if it were part of the dance, Morgiane drew the sword from its sheath.

Ali Baba was delighted. He let her dance for a long time, thinking to entertain his guest who was actually waiting for the right moment to kill him.

As was the custom, when the dance was over, Abdalla took the hollow tambourine to collect some money.

Ali Baba threw in one gold piece, and the leader of the thieves took out his pouch to find one too. While he was fumbling in his pouch, Morgiane thrust the sword deep into his heart.

He died instantly.

Once again, Morgiane had uncovered the evil plot of the thieves' leader, and Ali Baba was determined to reward her richly.

A few days later, a magnificent feast was held to celebrate the wedding of his son and Morgiane.

Ali Baba let an entire year pass by, then as there appeared no reason to fear further reprisals, he mounted his horse and rode to the thieves' cave.

He cried out loud the words, "Open, Sesame!"

The door opened and Ali Baba found all the treasure as he had last seen it. Now he was the only one who knew the secret. He loaded his horse with gold and returned home.

At last he called his son and told him of his adventures from beginning to end, including the magic words.

And so this was how Ali Baba and his offspring passed the secret on from father to son. They lived in great splendor to the end of their days, and they were loved and honored by the entire city.

The Little Tailor

One summer morning, a little tailor was sitting cross-legged on his table near the window, sewing cheerfully. As he was working, a peasant woman came down the street, crying, "Jam for sale! Good jam for sale!"

The tailor thought this sounded very good, especially as it was almost lunch time.

He put his friendly face out of the window and said, "Over here, good woman. I would like to buy some jam."

The woman walked up the steps of the tailor's shop with her heavy basket and laid out all the jars she had in front of him.

It took a while for the tailor to examine them all, but he finally said, "This jam seems good. Measure two large spoonfuls for me, good woman; no – make it four!"

The woman had hoped for a better sale than this after letting him look at every single jar, but nonetheless gave him what he wanted.

When she had gone, the tailor took a loaf of bread out of the cupboard and cut a thick slice on which to spread the jam.

"That looks delicious," he thought, "but before sinking my teeth into it, I'd better finish sewing this jacket."

He put the bread down next to him on the bench and continued to sew. But the smell of the jam attracted some flies which were on the wall, and soon several of them had settled on the sticky sandwich.

"Who invited you?" exclaimed the tailor, trying to swat them. The flies took no notice of his flailing arms and buzzed around the jam in even greater numbers than before.

By this time the tailor had had enough. He grabbed a piece of cloth from the drawer and cried, "Just wait, I will give you what for!"

He struck out – and this time seven dead flies dropped to the counter.

"Good gracious!" he exclaimed. "I *am* a strong man. The whole city – no! The whole world must know about this."

Then he made himself a belt and embroidered on it in big letters: SEVEN AT ONE BLOW!

He put the belt around his waist and decided to go out into the wide world there and then.

Before he left, he searched the entire house to find something he could take with him, but all he could find was some old cheese, which he put in his pocket.

By the front door he noticed a bird that was entangled in the thicket. He rescued it and put it in his pocket with the cheese. Then he bravely took to the road, feeling as though he could walk forever!

After a while he passed by a mountain on top of which sat an enormous giant.

The little tailor went straight up to him and said, "Hello my friend. There you are, looking at the world below, and here I am on my way into the world to look for adventure. Would you like to join me?"

The giant gave him a scornful look and replied, "Funny fellow, you little shrimp!"

"Not I!" cried the little tailor.

He unbuttoned his coat and showed the giant his belt. "Read this, then you will know who you are talking to."

The giant read the words: SEVEN AT ONE BLOW! Obviously there was more to this little man than there seemed if he had killed seven men in this way. Still, he wanted to test him, so he picked up a stone and squeezed it so hard that water ran out of it.

"Do you have the strength to do what I have just done?" asked the giant.

"Is that all?" sniffed the tailor. "This is a child's game in my country."

He fumbled in his pocket and took out the old piece of cheese he'd brought from his house. Then he squeezed in his hand, hard, until the whey spurted out.

The giant could not understand how such a small man could be so strong.

He took another stone and threw it in the air, so high that it nearly went out of sight, and said, "Go on, little man, now you do that."

"A good throw!" said the tailor. "But the stone fell back to the ground again. I will throw one so high that it will never fall to earth."

He then took the bird, which he had rescued from the thicket, out of his pocket and threw it swiftly into the air. The bird was so delighted to be free once more that it flew swiftly up into the sky and out of sight.

"You can certainly throw," said the giant. "But can you carry as heavy as you can throw high?"

He led the little tailor to a huge oak tree which had been chopped down.

"If you are really that strong, help me to lift up this tree," he said.

"No problem," said the tailor. "Take the trunk on your shoulders, and I will take care of the branches and the top: they are much heavier."

The giant took the trunk on his shoulders and the tailor sat down on a branch behind. The giant then carried the whole tree by himself and, unknown to him, the tailor as well! He perched comfortably on a branch, merrily whistling a song, as if carrying a tree was a piece of cake.

After a few yards the giant, who was almost crushed by the heavy burden, could not take another step and cried, "Look out, I am going to drop the tree."

The little man sprang to the ground and seized the tree with both arms as if he had been doing his share all along.

"You are not all that powerful for a man of your size," he remarked to the giant.

The odd pair continued walking and soon they passed by a cherry tree, heavy with fruit.

The giant reached to pick some of the ripest cherries from the top branches where they were growing. Then he bent the branches down so that

the tailor could also eat some of the cherries.

The tailor was, of course, too weak to hold the branches down by himself. When the giant let go, the tree sprang upright, carrying the little man into the air with it.

When he fell back to the ground again the giant said, "What is the matter with you? Don't you have the strength to bend such a little tree?"

"This has nothing to do with strength," answered the little tailor. "Why, I jumped over the tree to save myself from the bullets coming from some hunters' guns who were shooting through the bushes. Couldn't *you* do it?"

The giant tried, but he could not jump over the tree and got stuck in the branches. So the tailor had the advantage over him yet again.

"Since you are such a sturdy man," said the giant, "I invite you to our cave to spend the night with us."

The tailor gladly accepted. When they arrived, they found other giants sitting around a fire, each with a roasted sheep in his hand.

The giant showed the little tailor a bed where he could lie down, but as the bed was much too big for his little body, he curled up in a corner.

At midnight, when the giant thought the tailor was fast asleep, he seized a huge iron bar and struck the bed in the middle, thinking to kill the little man.

The next morning, the giants got up early. They had forgotten all about the little tailor. When they saw him come out of the cave, very jauntily and rather impudently, they were overcome with fear, so they ran away into the forest as fast as they could.

The little tailor continued his journey, still with his head in the air. After a long day's walk, he arrived at a palace garden. As he felt a little tired, he stretched out on the grass and fell asleep.

Some people who worked in the palace found him. They inspected him from all sides and read on his belt: SEVEN AT ONE BLOW!

"Oh, why is this great warrior here in time of peace?" they asked themselves. "He must be an important lord."

They went to the king to tell him what they had seen. They told him that if war was to break out, this man would be very useful and that they should on no account let him go.

The king followed their advice and sent one of his courtiers to the little man to serve him as soon as he woke up. When the tailor opened his eyes and stretched out, the courtier at once offered him his services.

"I have in fact come for that purpose," said the tailor. "I am ready to accept the king's services."

He was welcomed with all kinds of honors and assigned an apartment in the palace, but the king's soldiers were jealous of him.

"What will happen if we have an argument with him?" they muttered to each other. "He will jump on us and kill seven at one blow. None of us will survive. We won't stand a chance!"

They decided to go to the king to ask him for permission to leave. "We cannot stay in the same place with a man who has killed seven at one blow," they said to him.

The king was distressed to see all his soldiers abandon him like this. He began to wish that he had never set eyes on the person who had caused all this trouble and said he was quite willing to get rid of the little tailor.

However, the king did not dare to dismiss him outright because he was too afraid that this fearsome man might kill him in order to seize the throne.

The king thought and thought, and at last came up with a plan. He had to make the little tailor an offer that he could not refuse as a great warrior.

Now, there were two huge giants who committed all kinds of crimes, who lived in the forest of this country. No one ever approached them without fearing for their lives. If the tailor were to defeat and kill them, the king promised to give him his only daughter as his wife and half his kingdom as well. He also gave him a hundred horsemen to help him carry out the task.

The little tailor thought that this was the chance

of a lifetime. He agreed to fight the two giants, but he did not need the help of the hundred horsemen, he said, because someone who has defeated seven at one blow is not likely to be afraid of just two opponents.

He set off for the forest at once, followed by the hundred horsemen. When he arrived at the edge of the forest, the little tailor told them to wait; he was determined to put an end to the two giants single-handed.

He went into the forest and carefully looked around him. In less than a second he discovered the two giants. They were sleeping under a tree, snoring so loudly that all the branches shook.

The little tailor filled his pockets with stones and climbed up into the tree at once. He crept along a branch which was hanging just above the two sleeping giants and dropped the stones, one by one, on one giant's chest.

It took a long time before the giant felt anything, but at last he woke up, shook his friend and said, "What are you hitting me for?"

"You are dreaming," said the other. "I haven't touched you."

They went back to sleep. The tailor then began to throw stones down on to the other giant.

"What is that?" he cried. "What are you throwing at me?"

"I haven't thrown anything at you. You must have been dreaming," answered the other.

They began to argue, but they were too tired to carry on for long and, after a while, went back to sleep.

However, the little tailor continued to play his game, this time dropping even bigger stones.

"That is enough!" cried the giant.

He jumped up like a madman and flew at his friend, who fought back fiercely. The fight became so violent that they tore trees out of the ground to use as weapons, and they did not stop until both of them fell dead on the ground.

The little tailor then left his hide-out.

He drew his sword and thrust it into each giant. Then he went back to his horsemen and said, "It's over and done with. I have given both of them the finishing stroke. The fight was terrible; they even tore trees out of the ground to throw at me, but what good is that against a man who has killed seven at one blow?"

"Aren't you injured?" asked the horsemen.

"No," he said. "Not a hair of my head was touched."

The horsemen could not believe it. They went into the forest and, to their great surprise, they found the two giants covered in blood, with trees lying all around them.

The little tailor went to the king to claim his reward. However, the king regretted that he had made this promise and he tried to find another way of getting rid of the tailor.

"There is another task you must complete before I give you my daughter and half of my kingdom," said the king. "There is a dangerous unicorn which runs about these forests doing a great deal of damage. I want you to capture it and bring it to the palace."

"I am even less scared of a unicorn than two giants. Seven at one blow is my motto," declared the little tailor.

He took a rope and an axe, and went into the wood. He ordered the soldiers who accompanied him to stay at the edge of the wood.

Soon the unicorn appeared and charged towards the tailor, meaning to spear him with its horn.

"Easy, easy," said the tailor. "Not too fast!"

He stood still until the animal was almost on top of him, then he quickly dodged behind a tree.

The unicorn, running with all its might, pierced his sharp horn so far into the trunk that it was impossible to pull it out again, and so the beast was caught.

The little tailor left his hiding place and put the rope around the unicorn's neck. Then, with his axe, he released its horn that was stuck in the tree. Finally he took the animal to the king.

The king was amazed that he had captured the unicorn, but still he would not give the tailor his reward. Instead he made a third demand of him.

The tailor was ordered to capture a wild boar that was rampaging in the nearby woods. The man could, of course, have the assistance of the king's huntsmen. The king was convinced that this time the little tailor was sure to fail.

Although he saw right through the king's plans, the tailor accepted this third demand, saying that it was merely child's play.

As before, he went into the forest alone, refusing help from the huntsmen. They were not angry with his decision because the boar had more than once got the better of them, and had killed or injured several of their number in past hunts.

The tailor strolled along the path and it wasn't long before he encountered the boar.

As soon as the boar saw him it charged at him, foaming at the mouth and snapping its sharp teeth that could easily bite through him. The nimble man rushed into a nearby chapel and immediately jumped out of the window at the far end.

The boar rushed in after the tailor, but within two leaps the tailor ran around the outside of the chapel and slammed the door shut behind him. The furious beast was caught, for it was too big and heavy to escape through the window.

Then the tailor went to the king, who was now obliged to keep his word and give the man his daughter and half his kingdom. If he had known that his son-in-law was a mere needleworker and not a great warrior he would have been outraged. The marriage was celebrated with much pomp, but little joy, and the little tailor became king.

One night, the young queen heard her husband talking in his dreams.

"Hurry up, apprentice, finish that jacket and patch those trousers, or I will give you a good whack," he was muttering.

She realized that the young man was not all he seemed and, listening closely, she soon discovered that he had been brought up in a tailor's shop.

The next morning she went to her father and complained. She begged him to release her from her husband who was only a humble tailor.

The king promised that he would help her.

"Leave your room unlocked tonight," he said. "My soldiers will guard the door and, when the tailor is fast asleep, they will come in and chain him up. Then they will take him to a ship that will carry him far away."

The young woman was delighted, but the king's footman, who had heard everything and who had grown to like the new heir, told him their plans.

"I will soon put a stop to that," the tailor said to him.

That evening he went to bed as usual. When his wife thought he was fast asleep, she got out of bed to unlock the door and then returned to bed.

The little man, who was only pretending to be asleep, began to cry out, "Hurry up, apprentice, finish that jacket and patch those trousers, or I will give you a good whack. I have defeated seven at one blow; I have killed two giants, chased a unicorn and captured a boar. Do you think I am afraid of the people that stand outside my door?"

When they heard this, the soldiers were overcome by fear and ran away as if the devil was on their backs. From then on no one ever dared to cross him and the tailor remained king for the rest of his life.

Tom Thumb

One evening, a poor farmer sat by the hearth poking up the fire to stir up some warmth. His wife sat next to him spinning thread.

"How sad it is that we don't have children!" he said. "Here it is always so quiet, while in the other houses it is noisy and lively."

"That is true!" sighed his wife. "If we only had one child, even if it were very tiny and not much bigger than my thumb, we would be satisfied and love it with all our hearts."

Now, it so happened that the wife's wish was granted. After seven months passed she gave birth to a child who was perfect in every way except that he was no bigger than her thumb.

"It is as we had wished it to be," she said. "He will be our dear child."

And because of his size, they named him Tom Thumb. Although he was given plenty of food, Tom did not grow any bigger, but stayed the same size as the day he was born. However, he had lively eyes and succeeded in everything he did because he was very intelligent.

One day the farmer was getting ready to go into the forest to cut wood.

"I wish that there was someone who could bring the cart to me," he said to himself.

"Oh father, I will take care of it," cried Tom Thumb. "You can rely on me! The cart will arrive in time in the forest."

The man started to laugh and said, "How can that be done? You are too small to lead the horse by the reins."

"That doesn't matter, father!" replied the lad. "If mother will harness it, I will sit in the horse's ear and tell him where to go."

"Well, we will give it a try." said the man.

When the time came, the mother harnessed the horse and placed Tom Thumb in its ear. From there he started to shout at the horse, telling it where to go – sometimes "Ya!" and sometimes "Wah!" He handled the horse as if he were a rider, and the cart went straight to the forest.

Just as the horse was turning a corner, and Tom Thumb was shouting, "Ya! Ya!" two strangers stood in his path.

"Well, what have we here?" said one. "The cart is moving, the horse is moving, but we don't see anyone leading it."

"There is something not quite right here," exclaimed the other. "Let's follow the cart to see where it stops."

The cart drove on to the forest and arrived at the exact place where the wood had been cut.

When Tom Thumb saw his father, he cried, "You see father, here I am with the cart. Now put me on the ground."

The father held the reins with one hand, and with the other hand he took his son out of the horse's ear. The little boy sat down happily on a straw.

When the two strangers saw Tom Thumb, they were so surprised that they did not know what to think.

Then one of them took the other aside and said, "Listen, this little fellow could make us a fortune if we exhibited him for money in a large city. We have to buy him."

Then, turning to Tom's father they said, "Sell us this little man. He will be well looked after."

"No," replied the father, "he is the apple of my eye and I would not sell him for all the gold in the world."

But hearing this proposal, Tom Thumb climbed up the folds of his father's coat, sat on his shoulder, and whispered in his ear, "Father, sell me today. I will soon return home again."

So, after a little more talk, his father sold him to the men for a large sum of money.

"Where do you want to sit?" asked the men.

"Oh, just put me on the rim of your hat. Then I can walk to and fro and look at the countryside without falling off," replied Tom Thumb.

They did as he asked, and when Tom had said goodbye to his father, they set off together.

They travelled until darkness came, and Tom Thumb then said, "Put me on the ground for a while."

"No, stay up there for now," answered the one who carried him. "It makes no difference to me."

"No," answered Tom Thumb. "I know my manners. Put me on the ground, quickly."

The man took his hat off and placed him on the ground near the road. Tom jumped into the thick undergrowth, then suddenly slipped into a mouse-hole that he had noticed beforehand.

"Goodbye, gentlemen, you can continue your journey without me!" he jeered as he disappeared.

The men ran towards him and prodded in the mouse-hole with their sticks, but it was all in vain. Tom Thumb crept further in, and as it was becoming dark, they could do nothing but return home, angry and with empty pockets.

When Tom Thumb could no longer hear their voices, he came out of the hole.

"It is dangerous on the ground when it is dark," he said to himself. "I could easily break an arm or leg. I'd better look for somewhere to rest."

Fortunately, he found an empty snail shell.

"Thank Heavens!" he said. "I can spend the night in here safely." And he crept into the shell.

A little later on, when he was about to fall asleep, he heard two men pass by.

One of them said, "How shall we set about stealing the rich pastor's silver and gold?"

"I could tell you that," Tom Thumb shouted.

"What was that?" said one thief, trembling. "I heard a voice."

They stopped to listen, while Tom Thumb continued, "Take me with you. I will help you."

"But where are you?" they cried.

"Look on the ground and listen where the voice comes from," he answered.

The thieves found him at last and picked up the snail shell.

"Listen, little fellow, how do you think you can help us?" they said.

"Oh, I can climb into the pastor's room between the window bars, and hand out to you everything you want," replied Tom Thumb.

"Well, we will see what you can do," they decided.

Soon they arrived at the pastor's house and Tom Thumb slid into the room through the bars.

When he was inside he started to cry aloud with all his might, "Do you want everything here?"

The thieves shuddered and told him, "Shhhh! Talk softly so as not to wake anyone."

But Tom Thumb pretended not to hear them and continued to shout, "What do you want? Do you want everything in here?"

The cook, who slept in the room next door, heard the voices. She sat up in bed and listened, but the two frightened thieves had run off.

After a while, when they had regained their courage, they said to each other, "The little fellow is trying to get the better of us."

They went back to the house and whispered, "Come on, be serious, and pass us something."

So Tom Thumb started to shout again as loud as he could, "Yes, I will give you everything. Come a little closer and put your hands inside."

The cook jumped out of bed and the frightened thieves ran away as if the devil was on their heels.

When the cook went into the room, she could not see anything. She put the light on and checked every corner of the house, but she did not discover Tom Thumb. So she went back to bed, thinking she must have dreamed everything.

Tom Thumb slipped out of the house and hid in the barn. He climbed into a pile of hay and found a cosy place to sleep.

He planned to rest there until the next morning, then return to his parents, but there were still other adventures in store for him. The world can bring a lot of trouble and bad luck, as Tom would find out next day!

As she did every morning, the cook got up at the crack of dawn to feed the animals. First, she went to the shed where she took an armful of hay

from the exact place where Tom Thumb was sleeping. He was sleeping so soundly that he felt nothing. In fact, he did not wake up until he was in the cow's mouth after she had taken a bite of the hay.

"Oh dear," he cried, realizing his danger. "How did I end up here?"

The only way to avoid being crushed by the cow's teeth was to slip down into her stomach, which the tiny lad bravely did. The cow didn't even notice and carried on eating.

"They forgot to put windows in this little room," he said when he landed in her dark insides. "The sun doesn't shine in and it would be difficult to get a candle in here."

Tom was very unhappy in his new 'home', especially as more hay kept arriving. The space around him grew smaller and smaller.

In a panic, he started to shout as loudly as he could, "Don't give me any more hay! Don't give me any more hay!"

The cook was milking the cow when she heard the voice shouting, but she could not see anyone although she looked. So she carried on, until Tom cried out again.

Suddenly she recognized the voice from the night before and she was so shocked that she fell from the stool and spilled all the milk.

She rushed to her master and cried, "Ah! Goodness! Pastor, the cow has been talking!"

"You are mad!" answered the pastor, who nonetheless went himself to the stable to see what was happening for himself.

As soon as he had set foot in the stable, Tom Thumb started to shout again, "Don't give me any more hay! Don't give me any more hay!"

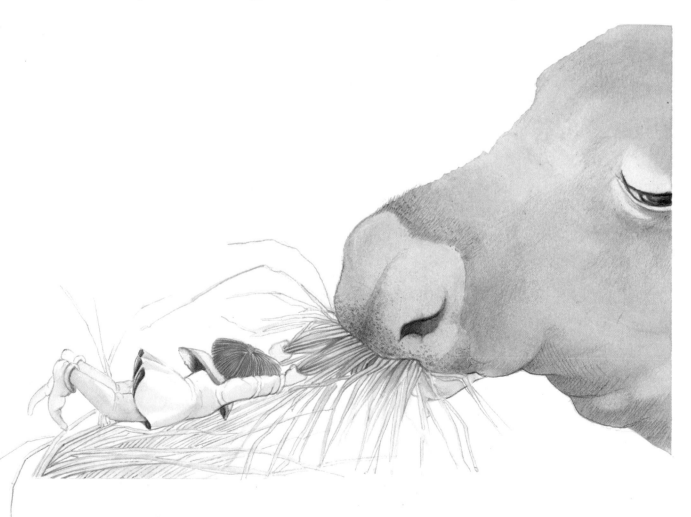

Then the pastor became frightened. He thought it was the voice of the devil, and he ordered that the cow be killed.

So the cow was slaughtered and they threw the stomach with Tom Thumb in it on the rubbish heap.

Tom thought that now he would be able to escape but, just as he managed to put his head out, another misfortune happened.

A hungry wolf that was passing by, swallowed the whole stomach in one gulp. Still, Tom Thumb did not lose courage.

"Maybe the wolf will listen to what I have to say," he thought. And from the wolf's belly he called, "Dear wolf, I know a delicious treat that you will find most enjoyable!"

"Where can I find this?" answered the wolf, although he found it odd to hear a voice from his stomach.

"I will take you there. You will find cake, bacon, sausages – as much as you can eat." Then Tom described his father's house in detail.

The wolf didn't need telling twice. That night, he found his way to the house and slipped into the kitchen through a hole in the wall. He slunk into the pantry where he ate and ate and ate.

When he had eaten his fill he tried to leave through the hole, but he had grown so fat that he could not go out the same way as he had come in. Tom Thumb then began to make a terrible uproar in the wolf's stomach.

"Will you be quiet!" said the wolf, groaning. "You will wake up the people who live here."

"Oh, too bad!" replied Tom. "You have eaten your fill! I want to enjoy myself as well." Then he began to yell and cry again with all his might.

At last his parents were woken up by all the noise. They ran into the kitchen and looked around. When they saw the wolf, the man fetched his axe and the woman grabbed a knife.

"Stay behind me," said the man. "I will hit the wolf, then you cut him into pieces."

When Tom Thumb heard his father's voice, he cried, "Dear father, I am here. I am in the wolf's stomach!"

"Goodness!" said his father. "Our dear boy has found us again. But what a way to return home!"

He told his wife to put down the knife because he was afraid it would harm Tom Thumb in the wolf's stomach. Then he gave the wolf a hard blow on the head which killed him.

Tom's father picked up a pair of scissors, cut the wolf's stomach open and rescued his son.

"Thank goodness!" he said. "We have been so worried about you."

"Yes father, it is good to breathe fresh air again," replied his son.

"Where have you been then?" asked the man.

"Ah! father, I have seen much of the world. I have been in a mouse-hole, in a cow's stomach and in a wolf's belly. Now I am home with you which is where I want to stay."

"And we will never sell you again, not for all the treasures of the world," declared his parents.

They hugged their sweet Tom Thumb for a long time. And from that day on, Tom was far more careful about the journeys he made.

Aladdin
and the Magic Lamp

In the capital of an oriental kingdom lived a young boy called Aladdin. He was poorly dressed and he spent his days running barefoot through the streets with other rascals. He had lost his father, and it was his mother who had the job of feeding him. She earned money for food by spinning from sunrise to sunset.

"One day I will be old," she often said to him, "and you will have to work to earn your living. So learn a profession!"

But Aladdin laughed. "A profession? There's plenty of time for that! I'd rather enjoy myself!" And he ran outside to find his friends again.

Now, one afternoon, when he was playing in the town square, a man approached him. He was a stranger and, although Aladdin didn't know it, a great magician.

He said to the boy, "Would you like to become rich?"

"Of course!" said Aladdin. "But one has to work to earn money, and I prefer to play."

The magician smiled, "Work? What a thought! Be like me and you will have more treasures than a king!"

Aladdin trusted the magician and went with him.

First the man took Aladdin to a clothes merchant where he bought a magnificent outfit for him: a jacket embroidered with gold thread, a pair of shoes and a fur hat. In those days only the rich people wore such clothes.

"This is because you have to be smartly dressed to enter the place where I will take you," said the magician as Aladdin admired the outfit.

They walked for a long time, until they had crossed the entire city. Once they reached the countryside they finally stopped, right at the foot of a mountain.

Aladdin looked around at the vast garden overgrown with bushes and was puzzled. "Is it really necessary to be dressed in silk to come here?" he said.

"Wait and see…," answered the magician.

He then took his time to light a fire which he sprinkled with incense from a glass bottle. A thick blue smoke filled the sky as he called out, "Come down, loyal spirit, and reveal your secret!"

Suddenly, Aladdin felt the ground trembling under his feet and he was terrified. He jumped back and there, right in front of him, the ground opened up. In the opening lay a square stone with a big iron ring.

"It is your turn to play now," said the magician. "This stone is magic, and you are the only one who can lift it. Beneath it you will find an enchanted orchard."

"It is much too heavy!" complained Aladdin, who was having second thoughts about the whole affair.

"Listen," said the man, "if you call out loud the name of your grandfather and your father while you pull the ring, you will have no problem lifting the stone."

The boy did as he had said... and lifted the stone. But instead of an orchard he saw a staircase which led to a dark cave. It made him shiver.

The magician explained to him, "The orchard is much farther away. First you have to go down the staircase, then across three halls and finally out again by another staircase. As you can see, the stairway is too small for me. Only you can go through it. But be very careful not to touch the walls as you go, or you will be struck by a bolt of lightning!"

Aladdin was still scared, but the magician gave him a ring and said, "This will act as a charm to protect you. If you do as I have said, you have nothing to fear. The second staircase leads to the orchard where you may pick all the fruit you want. But the most important thing that I want is a little lamp hidden in a secret place at the back of the orchard. Bring it to me!"

Aladdin hesitated, but the man pushed him inside. He went down the stairs slowly, step by step, holding his clothes tightly around him, terrified that he might accidentally touch something and be struck by lightning.

When he reached the foot of the stairs he crossed the three large halls without any difficulty. The last of these led him to the foot of a second staircase. Aladdin started to climb this staircase and eventually saw a light coming from the top.

Encouraged, he began to hurry…

When he reached the top he found himself in a fantastic garden with hundreds of trees full of shining fruit! However, this fruit was not meant for eating: the trees were laden with precious stones, sparkling diamonds, rich red rubies and milky pearls.

Poor Aladdin thought they were made of glass, like the cheap jewelry his mother wore. Nevertheless, he decided to pick some for her and began to fill his pockets. Then he saw the lamp standing in a hollow rock, and he remembered the reason for his visit. He stopped picking and ran towards it.

Lamps like this were to be found by the thousand in the East in those days and Aladdin did not understand why the magician wanted this one.

When he made his way back he found the stranger where he had left him.

"Do you have the lamp? Perfect!" the man cried.

Then he held out his hand and said, "Now give it to me. It will be much easier for you to climb the last few narrow steps without the lamp."

Aladdin saw the man's eyes light up with such greed that he did not trust him.

"No thank you, I can manage perfectly well!" he answered.

The magician insisted, but when he saw that Aladdin was not so easily led, he became very annoyed.

"How dare you disobey me!" he angrily. "This will cost you dearly!"

He poured the rest of the contents of the glass bottle over the fire and uttered some words that made the ground tremble. Before Aladdin could even go one step further, the opening closed!

The boy ran as fast as he could back to the stairs that led to the orchard, but that way was closed too!

"I have been caught like a rat in a trap!" groaned the boy, and collapsed on the stairs in tears.

Certain that he was destined to die all alone in this black hole, Aladdin fell asleep. For how long? That was difficult to say since no daylight came in.

When he woke up he was starving hungry and very cold. He rubbed his hands together to warm them up. As he was doing so, he also rubbed the ring that the magician had given him.

It did not take much rubbing before an extraordinary figure suddenly appeared from the ground. With his crooked hands, his long moustache and his dark eyebrows, he looked very fierce.

Nevertheless he said, "I am the genie of the ring. Your wish is my command. What do you want?"

"I want to get out of this place!" exclaimed Aladdin.

As soon as he made his wish, it was granted. The genie vanished and the cave opened. Aladdin was delighted and leapt outside, as free as a bird! Then, without losing any more time, he rushed home.

When his mother saw Aladdin she cried out with joy, "My child! My darling! I thought you were dead! Where have you been all this time?"

Aladdin told her what had happened to him and showed her the lamp, as well as the precious stones. His mother also thought they were made of glass. She did not give them another thought and put them in a box where they lay forgotten.

As for the lamp, she decided to sell it. Her starving son had eaten all the food in the house and with this she could buy some more bread.

She took a rag and polished the lamp... But two seconds later she dropped it on the floor and stared. A curious figure was standing in front of her, as terrifying as a demon. Nevertheless, when he spoke he sounded very friendly.

"I am the genie of the lamp," he said. "Tell me your wishes and they will be granted."

But it was Aladdin who spoke first: "We want something to eat!"

As soon as his wish was made, it was granted. The genie brought bread, two bottles of wine and all sorts of succulent food served on silver plates. There was enough for at least four meals!

Believe me, that night Aladdin and his mother went to sleep with full stomachs. And now that they knew how to make the genie appear, they were able to ask for everything they wanted. A soft touch with a rag on the lamp of happiness and, two minutes later, dinner was ready!

Soon they had more plates, forks and spoons than they knew what to do with, so they decided to sell them. They were made of silver, so they sold them for a good price. At last Aladdin and his mother had found a way to earn their living without getting tired!

The genie and the lamp kept them well for many years. As Aladdin grew up he lost his lazy attitude and took an interest in learning new things.

The rich merchants with whom he did business taught him good manners and the art of distinguishing glass from diamond.

At last he realized that the colourful fruits from the orchard were precious stones, and that he and his mother were, in fact, rich!

He was still counting all his wealth and wondering how to spend it, when something happened to interrupt his thoughts: Badroulboudour, the eldest daughter of the sultan and a princess of high rank, passed by his house.

Followed by her servants, she went to the bath house. She was renowned as a great beauty but, with a fan in her hand and a veil over her face, it

was impossible to see whether it was true.

Aladdin, intrigued by the princess, followed her secretly. When they arrived at the bath house, Aladdin hid behind a door and stared. When the princess lifted up her veil the young man saw the most beautiful face he had ever seen. The next second he had fallen in love with her!

He ran home to his mother and told her everything. She thought he had gone mad, especially when he told her that he wanted to marry the princess.

"Marry her!" cried the good woman. "But her father is a rich sultan, and we, my child, are poor people!"

"Not any more!" replied Aladdin.

He went to look for the box in which lay the treasure from the orchard.

Taking it to his mother, he ran the jewels through his fingers and said, "They are real! Each diamond is worth more than all the silver plates we have sold. If you go to the palace with such a present, I am certain you will be admitted."

"To the palace!" cried his mother. "But I would never dare to do that! What would I say to the sultan?"

"That your son loves the princess and that he wants to marry her!" replied Aladdin. "Then you lay the present at his feet. Oh! I beg you, Mother, if you don't do it, I think I will die!"

Aladdin's mother was very frightened, but nonetheless she went to the palace the next day and knocked at the gate. She held the present close to her heart: a large cup containing precious stones and diamonds, covered with a white cloth.

She was reassured to see that she was not alone. Many people came to the palace, sometimes from afar, to ask the sultan for advice or a favor, and this happened almost every day.

After a while they were admitted, one by one. Aladdin's mother sat down in a corner and waited her turn. But when it came, she felt too shy to speak and ran away.

Aladdin groaned when he saw her come back, completely confused and still carrying the gift. She promised him that next day she would go to the sultan again.

Unfortunately, that day the sultan had gone out hunting and Aladdin's mother found the palace doors shut. Her son was so disappointed! He thought he was going to die of a broken heart!

The third day, however, his mother did get in to see the sultan. He received her as he was sitting on his majestic throne. Grandly he waved her closer and she bent down low to kiss his feet.

"What can I do for you, my good woman?" he asked.

The poor woman trembled and was too scared to talk at first.

"Come, come! What is it?" he urged.

"Your Highness," she finally said, "I am afraid that my demand will not please Your Majesty… It is so insane, so senseless…"

"I order you: talk!" said the sultan who was becoming impatient with curiosity. "Whatever you ask me, you will be forgiven."

"Eh, well you see," she said, "it is my son, Aladdin… he has seen… he wants to…"

But instead of finally admitting the truth, she lifted up the cloth that covered the diamonds, and said, "He wants to offer you this modest present."

The sultan was startled: he had never seen such wealth!

Aladdin's mother took advantage of this and suddenly added, "My son loves your daughter. He is deeply in love with her and wants to marry her!"

Then she looked down at her feet, sure that the sultan would be furious and send her away…

But not at all! The treasure had such an effect on the sultan that he said, "Tell your son that my answer is yes!"

It is not hard to imagine Aladdin's joy that evening when his mother returned home. He was going to marry the sultan's daughter!

But the next morning he received a message from the sultan which read:

"*If young Aladdin wants my daughter's hand in marriage, he will have to bring me forty bowls filled with precious stones, pearls and diamonds, carried by forty servants.*"

"He has changed his mind," said the mother to her son. "I knew this would happen – he has found out that we are really poor! He doesn't want to admit that he broke his promise, so he asks you for things that you can't give."

"Eh well, that remains to be seen!" replied Aladdin, and he immediately looked for his magic lamp.

As soon as he rubbed it, the genie appeared.

"What do you want?" he said, gruffly.

Aladdin told him and two seconds later, all the forty servants appeared.

The little house suddenly became overcrowded. The servants looked splendid in their brilliant clothes, and on their heads they carried large silver bowls, filled to the brim with diamonds!

Aladdin commanded them to go to the palace to lay their treasures at the princess' feet. Then he said to his mother, "Go with them. You will bring me the sultan's answer."

When she came back from the palace after an hour, the good woman was crying. Aladdin was scared out of his wits, thinking they had failed… but she soon put him right.

"Don't look so sad, you silly, these are tears of joy!" she cried. "When the sultan saw the servants arrive, he did not have a second thought and cried out: 'Someone who can offer me so much wealth is worthy to marry the most beautiful princess!' I am so proud of you, my son!"

Aladdin was thrilled. He embraced his mother and danced her around the room.

"There is one little thing that worries me," she said at last. "The sultan's grand vizier alone was not happy. His son also had hoped to marry the princess. You will have to watch this man carefully in the future."

But Aladdin did not listen any more. He took the magic lamp and rubbed it.

When the genie appeared he commanded, "I want to take a bath!"

He had hardly pronounced these words when he felt himself lifted by invisible hands and plunged into an immense basin overflowing with perfumed water. What a marvelous bath! How good he felt! He came out clean and soft from head to toe.

Then he was dressed in magnificent clothes. When his mother saw him she cried out because he looked so handsome.

"This is only the beginning," he said, smiling. "The genie has promised me a hundred servants and a horse! And for you, dear Mother, thirty loyal servants!"

As soon as he had said these words everything appeared.

Aladdin had never ridden a horse before, but he mounted without any difficulty, for the genie had thought of everything.

"To the sultan's palace," he cried, urging the horse forward.

The horse obeyed and everyone followed him.

The people who saw this marvelous procession pass by could not believe their eyes, especially when the servants began to throw gold pieces in the air!

"Long live Aladdin!" cried the crowd, picking up the money.

Then the palace doors opened wide before him.

The sultan welcomed him. He was not disappointed with the look of his future son-in-law and neither was Badroulboudour.

She looked at Aladdin from behind some screens and fell immediately in love with him. She was at that time forbidden to show him her face: according to the oriental custom in those days, she had to keep it veiled until the day they married.

Aladdin talked with her father. Everything went well, and the sultan invited the young man and his mother to a magnificent feast.

"Glory to you, Aladdin!" he said, raising his glass. "You are worthy of my daughter and I give you her hand in marriage! When do you want the wedding?"

"As soon as I have built a palace beautiful enough for her to live in!" answered the young man.

"Well spoken!" said the sultan, and he emptied his glass.

That evening, at home, Aladdin's mother declared, "Explain it to me, my son, because I don't understand. For all this time you have been dreaming about just one thing: marrying the princess. Now, just as your dream comes true, you destroy everything by making a promise you can't keep! Have you gone mad?"

"Not at all," answered Aladdin, picking up the magic lamp.

Before the genie even had time to speak, Aladdin had already made his wish: a palace entirely made of marble, worthy of the princess. It should have walls decorated with diamonds, mosaic flooring, finished with everything of the finest quality, and surrounded by magnificent gardens!

The genie listened, not the least surprised. When at last he spoke it was to ask, "And where do you want this palace to be situated?"

"Opposite the sultan's palace," answered Aladdin.

"Very well," said the genie. And with that, he vanished.

The next morning, the genie appeared and said to Aladdin, "Your palace is built. Do you want to visit it?"

The young man was stupefied with this speed, but he nodded and a second later he was transported to the palace.

It was exactly as he had commanded... but ten times larger, ten times more astonishing and more dazzling! When he went inside, Aladdin noticed that numerous people were already busy: room

maids, cooks, servants and guards. Everyone made a deep bow when they saw him pass.

He could see the sultan's palace from the front window. It was right across from his, as he had wished, with a long avenue in between. The princess could easily see her father every day, even after she was married. Aladdin was enchanted and thanked the genie warmly.

But someone in the sultan's palace wasn't pleased. Not the princess, of course, neither her nor her father. Indeed, when they woke up they both applauded at the sight of this miracle. No, the person who complained, protested, raged and sighed was the grand vizier.

"That palace isn't real!" he exclaimed to the sultan. "It is a magical trick! No one can build a palace in one night!"

"Magic or not, it's there!" replied the sultan. "Thanks to Aladdin who is rich and powerful! Whatever you think, he deserves the princess and he will marry her tomorrow!"

What was said was done. The marriage took place the next morning in the sultan's palace, and next evening the newly-weds moved into their magnificent palace across the way.

And so began a beautiful love story. The couple adored each other more and more every day, and Aladdin's mother, who lived nearby, got along very well with Badroulboudour.

Aladdin helped to govern the sultan's kingdom and, as time passed by, his subjects grew to love him more and more. Every time he went to the mosque or when he went hunting, he distributed gold pieces to the crowd. Everyone in the country spoke highly of his kindness, his generosity and his talent for keeping law and order.

He became so well known beyond the borders, the mountains and the seas that his name was even mentioned in Africa. There, lived someone who knew him very well, but who thought he had been dead for many years: the wicked magician!

He remembered the lad as if it were yesterday. If the poor Aladdin was rich now, it must be all thanks to the lamp he had found in the orchard. The magician promised himself to recapture it!

By means of magic he soon arrived in the East. There he swiftly disguised himself as a travelling merchant trading lamps. Then, finding out that Aladdin had gone hunting, he began to prowl around his palace.

As he was walking, he shouted, "Who wants to exchange an old lamp for a new one?"

Soon a window in the palace opened and a young servant appeared, waving a lamp. The magician recognized the magic lamp immediately. He was so happy that he left twelve others in exchange for this one. The servant called out many thanks, but the magician was already gone, carrying the lamp with him.

As soon as he was out of sight of the palace, he rubbed the lamp.

"Command, and I obey!" declared the genie when he appeared, for he had no choice.

"I want you to transport Aladdin's palace to Africa, as fast as possible," ordered the magician, "with everything inside and all the people that work in it!"

His wish was granted immediately, and just two minutes later the powerful genie flew off, carrying the magician, the palace and everything in it with him.

You can imagine poor Aladdin's face when he came home from hunting that night to find everything gone: no palace, no gardens, no furniture, no servants and, worst of all, no wife!

Frantic with worry, he ran like a madman to the sultan's palace.

"Ah, there you are, crook!" the sultan cried. "Where's my daughter? So, the grand vizier was right to curse your palace, saying it was just a magical trick! Well, my fine young beggar, you have forty-five days to redeem yourself. If my dear Badroulboudour still isn't back by then, you will be taken to the guillotine!"

Aladdin understood the sultan's anger and decided that he had better leave.

He crossed the entire city, looking everywhere for Badroulboudour, but no one had seen her. When he said that she had disappeared together with the palace, they thought he had gone mad.

He then went to the neighboring towns and, little by little, he searched the whole kingdom, but all in vain!

By the forty-third day, he was so tired and so desperate that when he saw a river, he decided to end it all. Just before he reached it, he slipped and fell.

Now, all these years he had been wearing the magic ring and forgotten all about it. When he fell, he rubbed the ring by accident and the genie appeared at once.

"Here I am, what do you want?" it asked.

"I want to see Badroulboudour again!" cried Aladdin.

The genie granted his wish on the spot. But to Aladdin's surprise, the genie took Aladdin with him to Africa.

There was his marvelous palace, stood like an immense green oasis in the middle of the desert.

He approached the nearest window and knocked on it gently. A few seconds later, the princess herself opened it!

She was so happy to see Aladdin again. She told him that she was a prisoner of the cruel magician who wanted to marry her against her will.

Aladdin was beside himself with joy to see her again. Nonetheless, he was confused.

"Why are you not surprised to see me here?" he asked.

"Last night I saw you in a dream," replied Badroulboudour. "Since then, I have been waiting for you. Come inside, I have a plan."

As soon as Aladdin was safely in the palace the beautiful girl told him her plan.

"At the moment the magician is not here," she said. "As soon as he comes back, you must hide. Tonight I will put a poison in his drink that a servant has bought for me. After that, it will be up to you to find us a way home again."

"That shouldn't be difficult!" cried Aladdin. "But first we will have to find a lamp that belongs to me and which must be in the hands of the wicked magician at this very moment."

He had hardly said this when a door slammed.

"There he is!" whispered Badroulboudour. "Quickly, hide yourself!"

Aladdin jumped into a clothes chest and she closed it after him. Time seemed to pass so slowly to the poor boy in his dark hiding place! Many questions went through his head, and he even wondered if Badroulboudour had miscalculated her plan. What if the deadly poison had no effect? What if the magician became suspicious and refused to drink?

The more the time went by, the more impatient he became and the faster his heart began to beat!

At last he heard footsteps and listened carefully. Did they belong to his wife or to the magician? Before he could give it another thought, the chest was opened: it was Badroulboudour! And she smiled at him!

"Come and see!" she cried.

He leapt out of the chest and walked behind her towards the dining room.

There he cried out with relief. The magician lay dead on the floor and the magic lamp stood next to him!

"I found it when I went through his pockets," explained the princess.

"Now, we are saved!" cried Aladdin.

Then Aladdin took the lamp and rubbed it. In less than a second the genie appeared.

"We want to return to our beautiful country!" cried the happy young man.

He had hardly pronounced these words when the palace and the gardens, the servants and the furniture, wife and husband, were all taken up by the powerful genie and flown back home.

When the sultan opened the grand palace shutters the next morning, a marvelous sight greeted his astonished eyes.

He was beside himself with joy when he saw that Aladdin's palace had returned. He didn't care a bit when the obstinate vizier repeated that it was just a magical trick, the sultan just hurried off to see his daughter.

Later on that day, a great feast was organized to celebrate Badroulboudour's and Aladdin's return, and if, amongst the laughter, one could sometimes hear some deep sighs, no one was surprised: it was only the grand vizier!

The Firebird

Far away from here, beyond three times nine countries in a three times ten kingdom, lived a tsar called Vislav. The tsar had three sons: the first one was called Vassili, the second one Dimitri and the third one Ivan.

The tsar's palace was surrounded by such a beautiful garden that no one in the world had ever seen one like it. In this garden grew all kinds of rare trees: trees with flowers and trees full of fruit. The tsar's favorite tree was an apple tree which grew golden apples.

At night, a marvelous bird always appeared in the garden. It was the firebird with golden feathers and diamond eyes. It would perch on the favorite tree, pick at the apples and fly away.

Tsar Vislav was distressed to see his wonderful golden apples disappearing day after day.

He called his sons and said, "My dear children, which one of you will catch the firebird? The one who catches it will receive half of my kingdom now, and inherit the other half after my death."

The princes cried, "Dear father! It will be our pleasure to try to catch the firebird!"

The first night, Prince Vassili went into the garden to watch for the bird. He sat down under the golden apple tree, but it wasn't long before he fell asleep. He did not hear the firebird come, and it ate a great many apples while he slept.

The next morning, Vislav called Prince Vassili, asking, "Well, my son, did you see the firebird?"

The prince answered, "No, my most royal father. It did not come last night."

The following night Prince Dimitri went to watch for the bird.

He made himself comfortable under the golden apple tree as his brother had done.

He stayed up one hour, two hours, then he fell into a sleep so deep that he did not hear the bird arrive either.

The next morning the tsar called Prince Dimitri, asking, "Well, my son, did you seen the firebird?"

"No my most loved, royal father, it did not come," replied Dimitri.

The third night Prince Ivan kept watch in the garden. He sat down under the apple tree and waited. One hour went by, then two, then three.

Suddenly the whole garden began to glow: the firebird had arrived. It perched on the apple tree and started to peck at the apples.

Ivan approached it so quietly that he was able to grab the bird's tail. However, he could not catch the marvelous bird; it slipped out of his hands and flew away. Only one single feather remained in his fingers.

The next morning, as soon as the tsar woke up, Prince Ivan went to his father and gave him the feather. It shone with such fire that it could have lit up a dark hall as well as a thousand candles.

Vislav was satisfied that Ivan had taken at least a feather from the beautiful bird and it was kept under guard in his palace. However, from then on, the bird never returned to the garden.

One day the tsar called his sons again and said, "My dear children, I give you my blessing. Set off to find the firebird. The one who brings it back alive will receive half of my kingdom now, and inherit the other half after my death."

Princes Vassili and Dimitri had been jealous of their younger brother ever since he had seized the marvelous feather. They left together, refusing to take Ivan with them.

He was all set to go by himself to search for the firebird, but his father said to him, "My dear son, you are young and not used to long and difficult journeys. Why don't you stay with me? I feel I am getting old. What if I died while all three of you were away? Who would reign in my place?"

Although the tsar was very anxious to keep his youngest son at home, in the end he had to let him go. Ivan asked his father for his blessing, chose a horse and set off on his quest.

He rode for a long time, a very long time. At last, one day he arrived at a huge grassland where there was a stone on which there was a strange message. It read:

The one who continues straight ahead will be hungry and cold; the one who turns right will stay sane and safe, but his horse will be killed; the one who turns left will be killed, but his horse will stay alive.

Ivan turned right. "As long as I stay sane and safe, I can easily replace my horse," he thought.

He rode for a whole day and then the following day. On the third day, he met a large grey wolf.

The beast said, "You have made it as far as here, Prince Ivan! However, you read on the stone

that your horse must die; this time has come."

Having said this, the wolf killed and ate the horse, then he disappeared.

Ivan was very upset at the loss of his horse. He wept for a while, then continued his journey on foot. He walked the whole day and then, overcome with fatigue, he sat down to rest.

The wolf joined him again and said, "I feel sorry, Prince Ivan. I'm sorry I ate your good horse and you are forced to walk. Come, climb on my back and I will take you where you wish."

Ivan explained to the wolf the purpose of his journey. Then the wolf began to run, faster than any horse. After some time, in the dark night, he stopped in front of a huge stone wall.

"Go on, Prince Ivan," the wolf said. "Climb up the wall. On the other side there is a garden where you will see the firebird. Take the bird, but don't touch the cage, or misfortune will befall you."

Ivan climbed the wall, delighted at the wolf's words. He took the firebird out of its cage, but then said to himself: "Why should I take the bird without its cage? How am I supposed to carry it?"

So he seized the cage, but at the same time a loud alarm echoed through the garden.

Immediately the guards woke up, caught Ivan and took him to the king, who was called Dolmat.

He was furious and shouted, "Aren't you ashamed of coming here to steal from me? Who is your father and what is your name?"

The prince answered, "I am the son of Tsar Vislav and my name is Ivan. Your firebird used to come to our garden every night and snatch golden apples from my father's favorite tree, stripping and damaging it. The tsar sent me to search for the bird. I have promised I would take it to him."

"Tell me, young prince, do you think you have acted honestly?" said Dolmat. "If you had come and asked me, I would have given you the bird. Instead you try to steal from me! If I were to spread the word in all the kingdoms about your behavior, what would they think of you?

"Now, listen Ivan, if you carry out the task I set you, I will forgive you and give you the firebird to take to your father. You must go to a far away kingdom. There you will find King Afron and take from him his horse with the golden mane. If you don't bring it back for me, I will tell everyone that you are a thief."

320

Sadly, Prince Ivan left King Dolmat, promising to find and bring to him the horse with the golden mane.

Ivan went and found his friend the grey wolf and told him what the king had said.

"Ah! Prince Ivan," said the wolf. "Why didn't you listen to me? If you had not touched the cage, none of this would have happened."

"I have made a big mistake!" admitted Ivan.

"Well, what is done is done!" said the wolf. "Climb on my back and I will take you where you have to go."

Ivan climbed on to the grey wolf's back and it set off as fast as lightning. After a long journey they arrived in King Afron's far-off kingdom.

The wolf stopped in front of the magnificent palace stables.

"Listen to me, Ivan," he said. "Go inside – the guards are all asleep. Take the horse with the golden mane, but don't touch the golden reins that are hanging on the wall or misfortune will surely befall you."

Ivan slipped into the stable. He was just about to leave with the horse with the golden mane when he saw the reins hanging on the wall.

The temptation to take them was so strong that once again he disobeyed the wolf. He took down the reins and immediately there was a deafening noise that woke up the guards.

They seized Ivan and brought him to King Afron who was very angry and asked, "What country are you from? Who is your father and what is your name?"

"I am the son of Tsar Vislav and my name is Ivan," replied the miserable youth.

"Young prince," said King Afron. "Does it suit a royal warrior to do what you have done? If you had come to ask me, I would have been honored to give you the horse with the golden mane. Instead you steal from me! If I were to spread the word in all the kingdoms about your behavior, what would they think of you?

"Now listen, Prince Ivan! If you carry out the task I set you, I will forgive you and give you both the horse with the golden mane and the golden reins. You must go to a kingdom far away and search for Princess Helen-the-beautiful. I have loved her for a long time, but I have not been able to win her heart. Bring her here, or I will lock you up as a thief."

Ivan promised King Afron that he would bring him the princess. Then he left the palace to rejoin the grey wolf.

"Ah! Young prince!" exclaimed the wolf. "Why didn't you listen to me? Why did you take the golden reins?"

"I have made another big mistake," said Ivan.

"Well, what is done is done!" said the wolf. "Climb on my back and I will take you where you have to go."

Ivan climbed on his back and the wolf left at full speed. After a long journey they arrived in the beautiful Princess Helen's kingdom.

The wolf set Ivan down in front of the golden gate of a magnificent garden.

Then he said, "Wait for me in the grassland under the big oak tree."

Ivan did as he was told, while the wolf remained in front of the golden gate. At sunset Princess Helen-the-beautiful, surrounded by her servants, went into the garden. When she passed close by the grey wolf he jumped over the gate, seized her and ran back to Ivan.

The wolf told him to jump quickly on to his back behind Helen-the-beautiful and they set off

at once in the direction of King Afron's palace.

During the journey, Prince Ivan and Princess Helen fell in love with each other. When they arrived at the king's palace, Ivan burst into tears!

"Why are you crying?" asked the wolf.

"Why shouldn't I cry, grey wolf, my dear friend? I love Helen-the-beautiful, and now I have to give her to King Afron in exchange for the horse with the golden mane."

"I have helped you through many difficulties and I will help you again," said the wolf. "I will change into the princess. You will take me to the king and receive the horse with the golden mane. When I know you are far enough away, think of me so I can turn back into a wolf and rejoin you."

Having said this, the wolf took the form of the beautiful princess.

The king was beside himself with joy when Ivan brought him the wolf disguised as Princess Helen-the-beautiful. Immediately he handed over the horse with the golden mane to the prince.

Then Ivan mounted this horse, took Helen-the-beautiful up before him and set off for King Dolmat's kingdom.

Ivan and Helen talked to each other as they rode, forgetting all about the rest of the world.

At last, Ivan thought, "Where is my good grey wolf?"

Suddenly the wolf appeared before him and said, "Climb on my back, Prince Ivan, and leave the horse with the golden mane to the princess."

The prince obeyed and they continued their journey to King Dolmat's kingdom. They stopped when they were three miles from the city.

"Listen grey wolf, would you do me a favour one more time?" asked Ivan. "It will be the last one. Would you disguise yourself as the horse with the golden mane for King Dolmat? I would so much like to keep him."

The grey wolf at once did as he was asked.

Then Ivan left Helen-the-beautiful in a meadow while he went to meet the king. Dolmat was overcome with joy to see Ivan on the fine horse.

He welcomed him gladly, then gave Ivan the firebird in its golden cage.

The young prince left the city to rejoin Helen-the-beautiful. They both climbed on to the real horse with the golden mane and took the road to Tsar Vislav's kingdom.

A little further on Prince Ivan thought, "Where is my good grey wolf?"

Once again the wolf caught up with them and invited Prince Ivan to climb on his back.

When they arrived at the spot where the wolf had killed the prince's horse, the faithful beast stopped and looked at the young man.

"I have been your loyal servant, Prince Ivan," he said. "It was here where I killed your horse, and it is here where I must leave you. Go now where you have to go, I will not serve you any longer."

The grey wolf disappeared and Ivan wept for a while because he was very sad to lose his dear friend.

Then Ivan and Helen-the-beautiful continued their journey.

They were almost at Vislav's kingdom when they stopped for a rest. They tied the horse under a tree, lay down on the soft grass and fell asleep. The cage containing the firebird stood on the grass next to them.

Now, while Ivan had been having his many adventures, Prince Dimitri and Prince Vassili had been wandering around endless kingdoms without finding anything. Now they were returning empty-handed to their father.

By chance the two cruel princes passed by the place where Ivan and Princess Helen were asleep.

When they saw the marvelous horse and the magnificent firebird they were overcome with rage and jealousy.

They attacked their brother, then woke up the beautiful princess, who was terrified.

Through her sobs, she cried, "I am known as Helen-the-beautiful. Prince Ivan brought me here. If you had been honorable warriors, you would have offered him a fair fight. But you have killed a man while he was sleeping. That is as despicable as striking someone who is unarmed."

Then Prince Dimitri threatened the princess with his sword.

"Listen, Helen-the-beautiful," he said, "you are coming with us to our father, the Tsar Vislav. You will tell him that we won you, together with the horse with the golden mane and the firebird. If you don't tell him this, we will kill you."

The two princes then drew straws to see which one of them would marry the princess. Prince Vassili won. He lifted her on to his horse, while Prince Dimitri took the golden cage and set off on the horse with the golden mane.

Prince Ivan, who had been left for dead by his wretched brothers, lay on the ground for thirty days. As luck would have it, the grey wolf came by and when he recognized the young prince he vowed to save his life. The wolf caught a crow and promised never to hurt it if it would fly to the sacred well, far away.

The crow flew away and eventually came back after three days. He carried with him a flask filled with magic water. The grey wolf sprinkled Ivan with the water.

At once the prince woke up and said, "Ah! I have slept for such a long time!"

"Without me you would have remained in an eternal sleep," said the wolf. "Your brothers have taken Princess Helen-the-beautiful, the horse with the golden mane and the firebird to your father. Now, hurry home because your brother Vassili is going to marry the beautiful princess today. Climb quickly on my back, I will take you there."

Ivan climbed on the grey wolf's back and they arrived soon at Vislav's palace.

His brother Prince Vassili, who was about to marry Helen-the-beautiful, stood beside her.

When Ivan entered, the princess ran towards him, embraced him and cried, "This is the man I am to marry. It is Prince Ivan, not the scoundrel who is with me at this table!"

Then Tsar Vislav stood up and questioned the princess who told him the true story. Vislav was enraged and threw his two elder sons into a deep dungeon.

Prince Ivan married Princess Helen-the-beautiful that very day. They lived in perfect harmony and never were parted again.

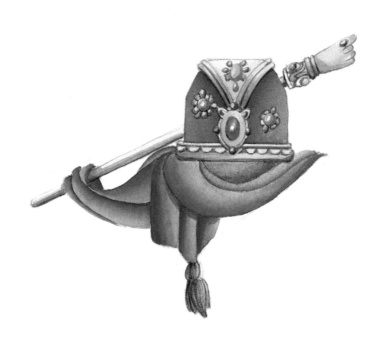

Ricky Tuftyhead

Once upon a time there was a queen who gave birth to a son, so ugly that it seemed doubtful whether he was human. A fairy who was present at his birth declared that everyone would like him because he would be very intelligent. She added that, by virtue of the gift she was going to give him, he could give as much intelligence as he had to the person he loved most.

All this consoled the poor queen a little and no sooner had the child started to talk, than he said a thousand nice words. In everything he did there was something very witty which people thought

very charming. I forgot to say that he came into the world with a little tuft of hair on his head, which led to his nickname, Ricky Tuftyhead.

Six or seven years later, the queen of a neighboring kingdom gave birth to two girls. The first girl was more beautiful than the day and the queen was delighted. However, the same fairy who had attended the birth of little Ricky Tuftyhead was present, and to bring her down to earth she declared that this little princess might be beautiful, but she would have no intelligence whatsoever!

This news upset the queen badly, but a few moments later she was even more shocked, for the second child she gave birth to was as ugly as the first was beautiful.

"Do not worry, Madam," said the fairy. "Your daughter will be so intelligent that her lack of beauty will almost remain unnoticed."

"So be it," answered the queen. "But is it not possible to give my elder daughter even a little intelligence?"

"I cannot do anything for her as far as intelligence is concerned," said the fairy, "but I will give her the power to make anyone beautiful whom she wishes."

As these two princesses grew up, their qualities grew with them, and everywhere in the land, the people talked about the incredible beauty of the elder princess and the astonishing intelligence of the younger.

It is also true that their faults progressed with their age. The younger princess became visibly uglier, and the elder became more stupid from day to day. Furthermore, she was so clumsy that she could not arrange china ornaments on the mantelpiece without breaking one, neither could she drink a glass of water without spilling half of it.

Although good looks may be a great advantage to a young person, the younger girl almost always had the better of her elder sister in any company. People always admired her, but they were always more interested in what the intelligent princess had to say.

Although the elder princess was quite stupid, she noticed this and was often very lonely. Indeed, she would have given all her beauty without a moment's hesitation in order to have even half the intelligence of her sister.

The queen, although she knew it was not fair, could not help reproaching her elder daughter for

her stupidity, which made the poor princess so unhappy she almost wished she were dead.

One day, when she had run into the woods to cry over her misfortune by herself, she saw a little man coming towards her. He was very ugly and unattractive, but magnificently dressed.

Of course, it was the young Prince Ricky Tuftyhead. He had fallen in love with the princess from her portraits that were spread throughout the world, and had left his father's kingdom so that he could see her and talk to her.

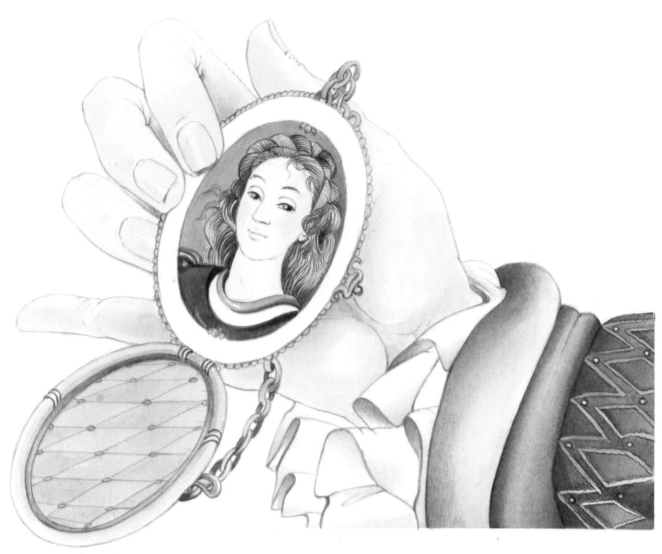

Delighted to meet her here all alone, he approached her with all due respect and all the politeness imaginable. After he had paid her the conventional compliments, he noticed that she was extremely unhappy.

"I do not understand how a princess as lovely as you can be as sad as you appear to be," he said. "I have seen countless numbers of lovely girls in my life, but I can tell you truthfully that I have never seen, in all my travels, one whose beauty compares to yours."

"It is very kind of you to say so, Sir," replied the princess.

Ricky Tuftyhead continued: "Beauty brings so many advantages that it is the most important gift of all, and if one has been given it, I do not see that there is anything to cry about."

"I would rather be as ugly as you are and be intelligent," said the princess, "than to have my beauty and yet be as stupid as I am."

"I cannot believe that you are stupid," said Ricky. "Indeed, often clever people don't believe they have any intelligence at all. I think it is the nature of that gift, that the more intelligent the person is, the more he thinks he is not."

"I don't know about that," said the princess, "but I do know that I am extremely stupid, and that is why I am so miserable I could die."

"If that is the only reason for your misery, I can easily put an end to your unhappiness," declared Ricky.

"And how would you do that?" asked the princess.

"I have the power to give intelligence to the person whom I love," he replied, "and as you are this person, I see no reason why you should not have

as much intelligence as it is possible to have, providing that you will marry me."

The princess was completely dumfounded and could not think what to say.

"I can understand," continued Ricky Tuftyhead, "why my proposal has confused you, and I am not surprised. So listen, I will give you a whole year to think about it."

The princess had so little intelligence, but at the same time desired it so much and, as the end of the year was so far away, she accepted the prince's proposal.

She had no sooner promised Ricky Tuftyhead that she would marry him on that same day the following year, than she felt completely different. Suddenly she found she could say everything she wanted, in a subtle, effortless and utterly natural manner.

At once she started to have a grown-up and entertaining conversation with Ricky Tuftyhead, in which she shone so brilliantly that he wondered if he had given her more intelligence than he had kept for himself!

When she returned to the palace, no one knew what to think of such a sudden and extraordinary

change. She talked as much sense now as she had talked nonsense before, and everything she said was extremely sensible and very witty.

The whole court was more delighted than you could imagine; only her younger sister was not happy with the change. Because she no longer had the advantage of intelligence over her beautiful elder sister, she merely seemed dreadfully ugly.

The king asked his advisers for guidance about how to deal with this new state of affairs and held council meetings in his apartments, but all in vain.

The news of this transformation having spread abroad, all the young princes of neighbouring kingdoms tried their best to win the heart of the beautiful and intelligent princess, and almost all of them asked for her hand in marriage.

In her turn, she did not find any of them intelligent enough, and she listened to them all without becoming attracted to any one of the hopeful suitors.

However, one day there came a prince who was so powerful, rich, intelligent and handsome that she could not help feeling attracted to him. When her father became aware of this, he told her that she was quite free to choose her husband without interference from him or his ministers, and that she only had to make up her mind.

The more intelligent one is, however, the more difficult it becomes to make a firm decision on such an important matter. After thanking her father for allowing her freedom of choice, she asked for some time to think it over.

It so happened that she went for a walk in the same forest where she had met Ricky Tuftyhead. She meant to consider in peace and quiet what she would decide to do.

While she was walking there, deep in thought, she heard muffled noises under her feet, as if several people were coming and going, and rushing around.

After listening more carefully, she heard them say, "Bring me that pot."

"Give me that copper pan."

"Put some wood on this fire."

At the same time, the ground opened up before her and she saw at her feet a huge kitchen full of cooks, kitchen boys and all kinds of people preparing a magnificent banquet.

A group of about twenty or thirty cooks left the crowded kitchen and went to a tree-lined path where they settled around a long table and started working to the rhythm of a song. The princess, amazed by this spectacle, asked them for whom they worked.

"Madam," replied one of the group, "we work for Prince Ricky Tuftyhead whose wedding takes place tomorrow."

The princess was even more surprised at that, but she suddenly remembered that this very day, a year ago, she had promised to marry Ricky Tuftyhead and she nearly fainted on the spot!

She had not remembered this promise because, when she made it, she was still a fool; but after Prince Ricky Tuftyhead gave her intelligence, she had completely forgotten all her rash promises.

She had not taken thirty steps further when Ricky himself bowed before her, elegant, magnificent and like a prince who was to be married.

"Madam," he said "I have kept my word, and I have no doubt you came here to keep yours – to make me the happiest man in the world by giving me your hand in marriage."

"I honestly confess," replied the princess, "that I have not yet come to a decision on the matter, and I doubt if I will ever be able to decide in the way that you wish."

"You surprise me," Ricky said.

"I believe you," she answered, "and, truly, if I had to deal with an unreasonable and stupid man, I would be very embarrassed. He would say that the word of a princess was her word of honor and that I should marry him because I had promised it. But since you are the most intelligent man in the world, I am sure you will understand.

"You remember that, even when I was a fool, I could not decide to marry you right away? The intelligence you gave me then has made me even more careful. So, how can you expect me to make a decision today which I could not make then?"

"If it is true that a man without intelligence would have the right to reproach you for breaking your promise, why then won't you permit me to do the same?" replied Ricky Tuftyhead. "Is it fair that people with intelligence are worse off than the ones with none? How can you agree with this, you who has so much, and who so greatly wished to have it?

"But let us get to the point, please. Apart from my ugliness, is there something else about me that displeases you? Are you unhappy with my birth and pedigree, my intelligence, my character or my manners?"

"Nothing at all", answered the princess, "I like everything about you."

"If that is true," continued Ricky Tuftyhead, "you can make me the most handsome man in the world."

"How can that be done?" asked the princess.

"It will be done," answered Ricky, "if you love me enough to wish it to happen. I know that at your birth the same fairy who gave me the power to give intelligence to the person I love, also gave you the power to make the one you love become beautiful."

"If that is the case," said the princess, "I wish with all my heart that you become the most handsome prince in the whole, wide world. I give you as much of this gift as I can."

No sooner had the princess pronounced these words, than Ricky Tuftyhead appeared in her eyes to be the most handsome, the finest and the most magnificent man she had ever seen.

Some people claim that the fairy's spell had nothing to do with this and that true love was the only reason for this change. They say that the princess marvelled at her lover's perseverance, on his discretion and on all the good qualities of his soul and his mind, and therefore no longer saw his deformed body, nor his ugly face.

They say that his hunched back seemed to her no more than the easy, cheerful manner of a man who shrugs his shoulders, and that where before she saw his awkward limp, it now appeared to her as if he just leaned in a rather charming manner.

They also say that his squinting eyes only seemed the more amazing to her, that their crookedness appeared to her to be a sign of the intensity of his love for her, and that his big red nose seemed to her quite manly and heroic.

Whatever the truth of the matter, the princess promised to marry him on the spot, provided he obtained the consent of her father, the king.

The king knew that his daughter had a lot of respect for Ricky Tuftyhead and, having heard from reliable sources that he was a very intelligent and sensible prince, he gladly accepted him as his son-in-law.

The wedding took place the next day, as Ricky had predicted, and according to the orders he had given that long year ago!

Beautiful Vassilissa

Once, in a kingdom far, far away, there lived a merchant and his wife. They had one daughter who was called Beautiful Vassilissa.

When the girl was eight years old, her mother became very ill. One day she called her daughter to her side.

"Listen, my child," she said, "and remember the last words I have to say. I am going to die, my dear. I give you my blessing and this little doll. You must always keep it with you and never show

it to anyone else. If ever you are in trouble, just ask the doll for advice."

Then the mother embraced her daughter and died.

The merchant grieved for a long time after his wife's death but, as time passed, he began to think about marrying again. He was a real gentleman and many women admired him. There was one widow of whom he was very fond. She had two daughters of about the same age as Vassilissa and was considered by everyone to be a good mother.

Then, one day the merchant married the widow, but he had been deceived because she was not a good mother at all to his daughter, who was the most beautiful girl in the village.

The woman and her daughters were extremely jealous of Vassilissa's beauty. They treated her very badly and made her do the dirtiest house-work, hoping that the hard work would make her pale and ugly.

However, Vassilissa did all the work without complaining, and every day she became more and more beautiful. Her sisters, although they never lifted a finger to help, became scrawnier and uglier because of their envy.

But how did this happen? It was all thanks to the doll that protected Vassilissa. It comforted her when she was unhappy, gave her good advice and helped her with the housework.

Several years passed by in this way until Vassilissa had reached the age to be able to marry. All the young men of the city asked for her hand in marriage, but no one ever thought about asking the other daughters.

Their angry mother always said to the suitors, "I will never consent to a marriage of the youngest daughter before the two older ones are married!"

Then, when she had driven away the suitors, she would turn and slap Vassilissa angrily.

One day the merchant went away on business to another kingdom. At once the woman moved into a different house near a dense forest. In the middle of this forest was a clearing with a small hut in which lived a witch. If anyone dared to come near the hut she would eat them, as if they were chickens!

The woman constantly sent Vassilissa into the forest on different pretexts, hoping the witch would rid her of the girl. But Vassilissa always

returned home safe and sound because the doll showed her the way home and warned her when the old witch was near.

One evening, the woman ordered all three daughters to do some work. One was to make lace, one was to knit stockings, and Vassilissa was to spin. Each of them had a certain amount to do

before going to bed. The woman then put out all the lights in the house, leaving only one candle burning for the girls. Then she went to bed.

The young girls started their work by this poor light. After a while the candle began to flicker. One of the sisters took a snuffer and pretended that she was going to trim the wick; instead she put the candle out on purpose.

"What are we going to do?" the girls cried. "There are no more matches to light the candle and our work is not finished. Someone will have to go to the old witch in the forest to ask for a light."

"I have enough light from my needles, so I won't go," said the one who was making lace.

"Neither will I," said the one who was knitting. "I have enough light from my needles too."

"You will have to go to find a light," they cried to Vassilissa. "Go to the witch."

Then they pushed Vassilissa out of her chair and told her to go.

The girl went into her room, gave some food to her little doll and said, "Dolly dear, eat this food and listen carefully to me. My sisters are sending me to the old witch and she will eat me."

"Don't be afraid," replied the doll. "Go where they send you, but take me with you and you will have nothing to fear."

Vassilissa put the doll in her pocket and walked bravely into the dense forest. As she was walking, a sudden breeze made her whole body shiver.

Then a horseman passed at full gallop in front of her; his face was completely white, and he was dressed all in white. To her surprise, it became light.

Vassilissa continued walking. Just then another horseman passed by her. This man's face was red, he was dressed in red and he sat on a red horse. To her surprise, the sun rose.

The girl walked on and on, until at last she arrived in the clearing where the old witch's little hut stood. It was circled by a fence made of human bones, and on top of the fence sat a row of skulls. On the door she saw a human bone which served as a bolt, and instead of a lock there was a human jawbone.

Vassilissa stopped walking for she was paralyzed with fear. Just then a third horseman arrived. His face was black and he was dressed in black, riding on a black horse. He rode up to the door of the old witch's hut and disappeared, as suddenly as if he had sunk into the earth.

Then it became night, but the darkness did not last for long because the skulls' eyes on the fence started to shine.

Vassilissa was still frozen with terror. She did not know what to do and stood there like a statue.

All at once there was a terrible noise in the forest; the trees shook their branches and the dry leaves rustled, and then the old witch appeared.

When she reached her doorstep, she stopped, sniffed the air and cried, "Mmmm! I smell a child! Who is it?"

Vassilissa went to the witch, curtsied and said, "It is I, Madam! My sisters have sent me here to ask for a light, for we have no matches at home."

"Good," said the witch, "I know them and I will give you the light. First, however, you must work for me for a while."

Then she turned to the door and cried, "My solid bolts, lift yourself; my door, open yourself!"

The door opened and the witch went inside, while the wind whistled through the house.

When she reached her room, the witch sat down at the table and said to Vassilissa, "Serve me everything that is in the oven, I want to have my dinner here!"

Vassilissa lit a candle by holding it against one of the shining skulls on the fence. Then she took the food from the oven and served it to the witch. She also went to the cellar to get some ale, beer and water. It was enough for ten men.

The witch ate and drank everything. All she left was a drop of cabbage soup and a small piece of bread.

Then the witch went to bed, saying, "While I am out tomorrow, you will clean the courtyard, sweep the rooms, make lunch and do the washing. Then you must go to the shed, where you will find a pile of wheat, and get rid of the beetles. Make sure that everything is done before I come home or I will eat you!"

When she had finished speaking, the witch fell asleep and began to snore.

Vassilissa gave the rest of the food to her doll, and in tears she said, "Dolly dear, eat this food and listen carefully to me. The old witch has told me to do an impossible amount of work and she will eat me if I have not finished in time."

The doll replied, "Don't be afraid, beautiful Vassilissa. Have your dinner and go to sleep. The night will bring an answer."

Very early the next morning Vassilissa got up and looked out of the window. The eyes of the skulls had stopped burning. Then the white horseman passed in front of her and it was light.

The old witch left the house and whistled. Her mortar, pestle and broom appeared at once. Then the red horseman rode by and the sun came out. The witch sat in her mortar and went off, driving

it with the pestle, while she swept away her tracks with the broom.

Vassilissa took the chance to walk around the house and admired the witch's wealth. She wondered what part of the work she should do first, but when she looked again, she noticed that the work was already done! And that was not all – the doll had removed the beetles from the wheat!

"Oh, my good helper," said Vassilissa "You have saved me!"

"You only have to prepare dinner, and there's plenty of time for that," answered the doll as she climbed back into Vassilissa's pocket.

In the evening, Vassilissa set the table and waited for the witch to return. When it started to get dark, the black horseman appeared in front of the door and immediately it became completely dark. Only the skulls' eyes glittered in the night.

Suddenly the trees started to shake and the leaves began to rustle. The old witch was coming. Vassilissa went to meet her.

"Is everything done?" asked the witch.

"Look for yourself, Madam!" replied the girl.

The witch looked around her. She was very annoyed that she could not find any faults.

"All right, Vassilissa!" she said. "This time you have done the work."

Then she cried, "My faithful servants, devoted friends, come and grind the wheat!"

Out of nowhere, three pairs of hands appeared, grabbed the wheat and took it away.

Once again the witch ate to her heart's content. Before she went to sleep, she said to Vassilissa, "Tomorrow you must do the same as you did today. However, you must also take the pile of poppies from the shed and wipe off the dust."

Having said this, she turned over to face the wall and started to snore.

As she had done the night before, Vassilissa asked her doll for advice.

The doll answered, "Don't worry, go to sleep. The night will bring an answer. Tomorrow you will see that everything has been done."

The next day, when the witch had left, Vassilissa and her doll once more shared the tasks.

When the witch came back that night, she was again annoyed to find no faults when she examined everything.

Then she cried, "My faithful servants, devoted friends, press the oil out of the poppies."

Out of the air, three pairs of hands arrived at her command, gathered the poppies and took them away. Then the witch ate her dinner, while Vassilissa stood in front of her in silence.

"Why don't you say anything?" asked the witch. "Have you lost your tongue?"

"If you allow me, I would like to ask you something," said Vassilissa.

"Ah! Ask if you like, but you should know that not every question leads to something good!" cackled the witch. "Remember, if you know a lot, you soon become old."

"I would like to ask you three questions," said Vassilissa. "On the way to your hut, I was passed by a horseman with a white face, wearing white clothes and riding a white horse. Who is this man?"

"He is my daylight," replied the witch.

"Then I saw another horseman who had a red face," continued the girl. "He was dressed in red and riding a red horse. Who is he?"

"He is my beautiful sun," answered the witch.

"And the black horseman I saw near the door?" finished the girl.

"He is my dark night," said the witch.

Vassilissa remembered the three pairs of hands, but did not ask anything more.

"No more questions?" asked the witch.

"I know enough for now," replied the girl. "You said yourself that a lot of knowledge makes you grow old too soon."

"That is true," said the witch. "I don't like

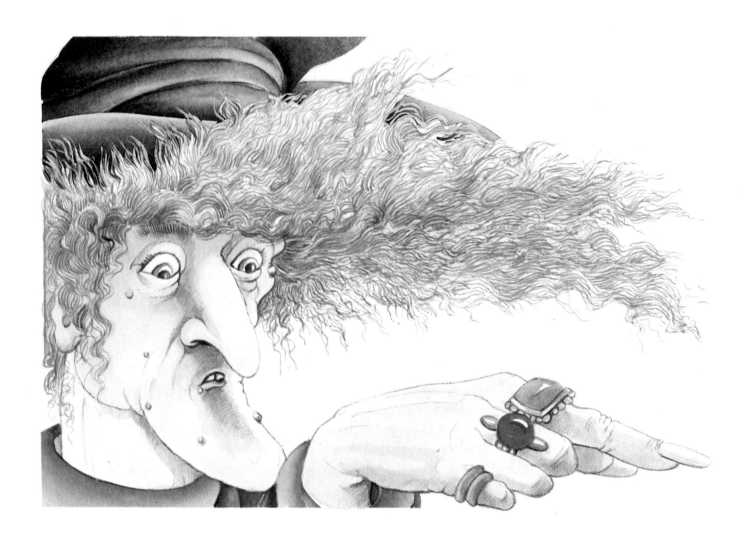

revealing my secrets to the world. But now, I will ask you a question. How did you manage to finish all the work I gave you?"

"My mother's blessing has helped me," answered Vassilissa truthfully.

"Ah! So that is the reason!" cried the witch. "Then you must leave this house at once, blessed girl. I don't like blessed girls!"

She grabbed Vassilissa's wrist and dragged her out of the room, then pushed her outside.

She then took one of the skulls with shining eyes from the fence, put it on a stick and gave it to Vassilissa.

"Take this, it's the light for your sisters," she said. "Take it home."

At once Vassilissa started to run and the light from the skull guided her.

After a long journey, she reached home again. When she went into the house, the skull said, "Don't throw me away, take me to the woman!"

For the first time ever, Vassilissa was welcome in the house. Since she had left, the woman and her daughters had been living in the dark. They had not been able to light a match, and any light they took from their neighbours went out as soon as they entered the room.

"Perhaps, your light will not go out," they cried, grasping the stick from her.

They carried the skull into the room and its burning eyes stared at the three women. It didn't matter where they tried to hide, it seemed that they were followed everywhere by its haunting look.

By the morning, they had all been burnt to ashes; only Vassilissa survived.

The next day Vassilissa buried the skull, locked the house and went to town to find work. An old lady asked for her companionship, and so she stayed there, waiting for her father to arrive.

One day, she said to the old lady, "I am very bored staying in the house all day with nothing to do. Please, buy me some flax and I will pass the time spinning."

"The old lady bought her some flax and Vassilissa began to spin. She worked so well that the thread came out as smooth and fine as a hair.

When she had spun a large pile of thread, Vassilissa wanted to start weaving it. The doll then gave Vassilissa a magnificent loom, suitable for weaving such fine thread. By the end of the winter, the cloth was finished and it was so fine that it could be threaded through the eye of a needle.

In the spring she bleached the linen and said to the old lady, "Please, sell this piece of cloth and keep for yourself whatever money it fetches."

"But my child," gasped the lady, "only the king is worth such a cloth! I will take it to the palace."

"What is it you want, dear woman?" asked the king when he saw her there.

"Your Highness," she answered, "Forgive me, but I have brought something wonderful to show to you."

When the king saw the cloth, he was also amazed. "What do you want for it?" he asked.

"Your Highness, this cloth is priceless," replied the lady. "I brought it as a gift."

The king thanked her and showered her with rich gifts in return.

"I would like shirts made from this cloth," declared the king. "But who can sew such finery?"

The king searched the land for such a needle-worker, but all in vain. Then he sent for the old lady again.

"If you have been able to spin and weave this cloth, you should also be able to sew it," he said.

"This cloth was not my work," she replied. "It was a young girl who made it."

"Well then, let her sew the shirts," ordered the king.

And so, the old lady went home and told the whole story to Vassilissa. At once she locked herself in her room and began to work night and day.

Soon a dozen shirts were finished and the good lady took them to the king.

It wasn't long before Vassilissa saw the king's servant standing at the door, saying, "His Majesty wants to see with his own eyes the girl who made his shirts. He wants to reward her in person."

Vassilissa set off for the palace and presented herself to the king, who, as soon as he saw her, fell head over heels in love with her.

He took beautiful Vassilissa's white hands and sat her next to him on the throne. That very day they were engaged to be married.

Soon afterwards her father came back from his long journey. He was delighted with his daughter's fate and made his home with her. Vassilissa also welcomed the old lady, who had given her shelter, into the palace and, of course, the dear doll stayed by her side forever after.

The Seven-League Boots

There was once a woodcutter and his wife who had seven children, all boys. The eldest was only ten and the youngest only seven. Everyone was very surprised that they had had so many children in such a short time, but it was because the wife had always born twins, except for the first-born.

The couple was very poor and their seven children were a great burden to them because none of them could yet earn his living. The youngest was extremely delicate and rarely said a word which made them very unhappy.

They thought he was stupid, but in fact he was really very clever. He was very small and, when he came into the world, he was no bigger than a thumb, which was the reason why he was called Thumbkin.

It seemed to the family that everything this poor child did or said was wrong. However, he was the finest and the most sensible of his brothers, and even though he talked very little, he listened a great deal.

Then came a very difficult year, when the land was hit by famine and these poor people had to make the decision to get rid of their children.

One evening, when the children were in bed, the woodcutter and his wife sat in front of the fire, talking.

He said to her, his heart broken with grief, "I cannot stand seeing our children starve in front of my eyes, so I have decided to lose them in the woods tomorrow. We will set them to gathering wood, and we will slip away without them seeing."

"Ah!" cried his wife, "could you really be so cruel as to lose your children?"

Her husband explained again how poor they were, but she could not consent to the plan.

However, after considering what a great grief it would be to see them starve in front of her eyes, she finally agreed and went to bed in tears.

Thumbkin had been listening to everything they said; he had got up quietly and slid under the staircase to be able to hear them without being seen. He went back to bed but could not sleep for the rest of the night, for he was thinking about what he had to do.

The next morning he got up very early and went to the bank of a stream where he filled his pockets with little white stones. Then he returned home.

When the family all left the house later, Thumbkin kept his secret to himself. Soon they were in a thick forest where it was impossible to see each other at a distance of ten steps.

The woodcutter started to work felling trees, while the children collected twigs and made bundles out of them. When their parents saw them working hard, they gradually moved away and then suddenly took off along a little footpath, which returned home by a different route.

When the children realized they were alone, they started to call for their parents and some began to cry.

Thumbkin told them not to cry for he knew
very well how to get back to the house. As they
had walked along, he had marked the path by
dropping the little white stones from his pockets.

"Do not be afraid, my brothers," he said. "Our
father and mother have left us behind, but I will
take you back home. Just follow me."

They followed him, and he led them back to
their home along the same path by which they
went to the forest that morning.

At first they were afraid to enter the house, and they put their ears to the door to hear what their father and mother were saying.

Now, when the woodcutter and his wife had returned home, they found that the Lord of the Town had sent them ten gold pieces. He had owed them the money for a long time, but they thought they would never get it back.

This had given them new hope, for the poor couple were indeed starving.

The woodcutter immediately sent his wife to the butcher's. Since she had not eaten for a long time, she bought three times as much meat than was needed to make supper for two.

When they had eaten their fill, she said, "Oh dear, where are our poor children now? They would have eaten a good meal tonight. I told you we would regret losing them! What are they doing now in that forest? Oh my goodness, perhaps the wolves have eaten them already! You are so cruel to have abandoned your children like that."

The woodcutter lost his patience as she went on for he was really just as upset as his wife. However, he never liked a person to say, "I told you so," quite as often as she did.

His wife was in tears now, and crying, "Alas, where are my children now, my poor children?"

She cried out so loudly that the children at the door heard her and started to shout all together, "We are here, we are here!"

She rushed to open the door and welcomed them with open arms.

"I am so happy to see you, my dear children!" she cried. "You must be very tired and hungry. And look how dirty you are. Peter, come here so I can wash your face."

Peter was their eldest son whom she loved the most because he was red-haired and took after his mother.

Then they sat down at the table and ate with a healthy appetite, which pleased their father and mother. While they ate they told their parents how frightened they had been in the forest, all talking at once most of the time.

The woodcutter and his wife were delighted to have their children home again but, alas, their happiness lasted only as long as the ten golden pieces did. When all the money was spent, they found themselves in the same desperate situation as before.

They decided that they had no choice but to abandon their children again. This time they planned to take them even further into the forest than the first time.

Although the parents talked very quietly, Thumbkin again heard their plan.

He thought that he would have no problem doing the same thing that he had done before, but when he got up early next morning to collect the stones, he found the door of the house locked.

At first Thumbkin didn't know what to do. However, their mother had given them each a piece of bread for breakfast, so he thought that he would be able to use this bread instead of stones. He would crumble the bread and drop the crumbs along the path, so he hid it in his pocket.

Once again the family set off. Their parents took the seven boys to the thickest and darkest part of the forest, and soon after they arrived made an excuse to leave them behind.

Thumbkin was not too worried because he thought he would find the way back easily, thanks to the bread he had scattered behind. But, when he looked, he could not find a single crumb: the birds had eaten every one.

This time the children were in a sorry state. The more they walked, the more they got lost and the deeper they went into the forest. Darkness came and a strong wind started to blow, which frightened them terribly. They thought they heard wolves howling and feared they would be attacked and eaten. They hardly dared to talk or move.

Then it began to rain heavily and they were all soaked to the skin. They slipped at every step and fell into puddles, from which they scrambled up completely covered in mud.

Thumbkin climbed a tree to see if he could discover something that could help them. Turning his head to look in all directions, he suddenly saw a tiny glimmer of light, like that of a candle, but it seemed to be far away beyond the forest.

He slid down the tree but, when he reached the ground, he could no longer see anything at all. Nevertheless, after walking for quite a while with his brothers in the right direction, he suddenly saw the light again and they came to the edge of the forest.

Finally they arrived at the house with the candle light. They knocked at the door and a woman opened it. Thumbkin told her that they were poor

children who had got lost in the forest, and he asked her if they could spend the night there for nothing, as they had no money.

Seeing how sad and handsome they all were, this women started to cry, saying, "Alas, my poor children, where have you come to? Do you not know that this is the house of an ogre, who eats little children?"

"Oh Madam, what should we do?" gasped Thumbkin, who was trembling with fear as well as his brothers. "The wolves in the forest will eat us tonight if you do not give us shelter. And if we are to be eaten, we would rather it was by the master of this house than the wolves. Maybe he would feel sorry for us, if you were willing to plead on our behalf."

The ogre's wife thought she might be able to hide them from her husband until next morning, so she let them inside and took them to the fireplace to warm themselves. It was very hot, and there was a whole sheep roasting on the spit for the ogre's supper.

Just when they began to feel warm, they heard three or four loud knocks at the door: the ogre had returned.

The woman quickly hid the children under the bed and went to open the door. The first thing the ogre asked was if the supper was ready and if a bottle of wine had been opened, and immediately he sat down at the table.

Suddenly he started sniffing to the left and the right and said that he smelled living flesh.

"It must be the veal which I was just preparing for you that you can smell," said his wife.

"I tell you, I smell living flesh," exclaimed the ogre and gave his wife a suspicious look. "There is something going on here, I think."

Having said this, he stood up from the table and went straight to bed. Then he realized what his sensitive nose had smelled.

"Ah, this is how you try to deceive me, you wretched woman!" he shouted. "I don't see why I shouldn't eat you as well, you old, stupid woman. These rabbits will come in handy to entertain my ogre friends who are going to visit me."

One by one he dragged the boys out from under the bed. The poor children fell on their knees and begged him for mercy, but they were in the hands of the cruelest ogre there ever was, who was already eating them in his imagination.

He told his wife that the boys would make a tasty stew when cooked in a nice sauce.

He picked up a huge knife and sharpened it on a long stone, then he approached the frightened children.

He had just grabbed one of them, when his wife said, "Why do you want to do it at this hour? You've had a good supper. Why don't you do it tomorrow morning?"

"Be quiet!" exclaimed the ogre, "they will be more succulent now."

"But you still have so much meat here," said his wife. "Look – a calf, two sheep and half a pig!"

"You are right," agreed the ogre. "Give them a good meal so they do not get thin, and put them to bed."

The kind woman was delighted and cooked the children a nice supper, but they were so terrified they could not eat a mouthful.

As for the ogre, he was so delighted to have such a delicacy to offer his friends that he drank a dozen bottles of wine, which made him dizzy and he had to go to bed.

Now, the ogre had seven young daughters. The little ogresses were all very robust and had ruddy complexions because they ate fresh meat like their father. But they had little round, grey eyes, hooked noses and huge mouths with long teeth, very sharp and very widely spaced.

They were not yet as cruel as their father, but were beginning to follow in his footsteps, for they already liked to bite little children.

They were sent to bed early and all seven of them slept in a large bed, each wearing a golden crown on her head.

In the same room there was another bed of the

same size. The ogre's wife put the seven little boys in this bed, after which she went to bed herself beside her husband.

Thumbkin was afraid that the ogre might regret not having cut their throats that evening and would wake up to do so before morning. He got up when he heard the ogre snoring, and took off his brothers' caps. Then he crept over to the ogre's seven daughters, took off their crowns and put the caps on their heads. He then returned to bed and put the crowns on his brothers' heads and his own.

It was just as Thumbkin feared; the ogre woke up at midnight and regretted not butchering the lads the evening before. So he jumped out of bed and took up his huge knife.

"Let us see how our little fools are doing," he said to himself.

Without lighting a candle, he groped his way upstairs in the dark to his daughters' room and approached the bed in which the little boys were sleeping. They were all fast asleep except for Thumbkin, who was very frightened when he felt the ogre's hand over his head.

The ogre felt all the golden crowns. "Dear me," he said, "This will never do. This is my daughters' bed."

He then went to the other bed and felt the boys' little caps.

"Ah, there they are," he said. "Our lively lads! Let's do the job properly now."

Having said this, he cut the throats of his seven daughters thinking it was the boys. Then, happy at a job well done, he went back to bed.

As soon as Thumbkin heard the ogre snoring again, he woke up his brothers. He told them to get dressed immediately and follow him.

The boys crept quietly out of the house and climbed over the garden wall. They ran through the night, stumbling from fear and not knowing which way to go.

When the ogre woke up next morning, he said to his wife, "Go upstairs and dress those little fools who came here yesterday."

His wife was very surprised at her husband's kindness, not suspecting for a minute that the way he meant her to dress them was as meat!

But when she went upstairs a terrible sight was awaiting her. She was horrified when she saw her

seven daughters with their throats cut, and fainted at once – even though she was an ogress!

The ogre wondered why his wife was taking such a long time doing the job he had ordered her to do. He too went upstairs and was no less aghast than his wife when he saw the dreadful sight, although he did not faint.

"Ah, what have I done?" he cried. "Those seven rascals will pay for this, and right now!"

First he revived his wife, then he shouted, "Quickly! Give me my seven-league boots so that I can catch up with those scoundrels."

Donning his magic boots, that would travel seven leagues in one stride, he searched throughout the land for the boys. After he had run a great distance in all directions, he finally came to the path where they were walking, no more than a hundred steps from their father's house.

To their horror they saw the ogre stepping from mountain-top to mountain-top, crossing rivers as easily as if they were small streams.

Thumbkin hid his brothers in a hollow rock nearby and then hid himself, peeping out to watch the ogre.

The ogre had become very weary from all his

travels, despite the seven-league boots (which are incredibly tiring to wear). He wanted to rest and by chance he sat down on the rock in which the boys were hiding.

After sitting there for a while he started to snore so frightfully that the poor children were just as scared as ever. Thumbkin told his brothers to run home as fast as they could while the ogre was sound asleep. They did as he said and arrived home almost immediately!

Then Thumbkin crept up to the ogre, carefully removed the seven-league boots and stepped into them himself. The boots were very long and wide but, as they were magic, they were able to grow larger or smaller to fit the person who is wearing them. So, when Thumbkin had them on they fitted his legs and feet perfectly, as if they had been made for him.

The little lad went straight back to the ogre's house where he found his wife weeping over her seven dead daughters.

"Your husband is in great danger," said Thumbkin. "He has been captured by a gang of robbers who are threatening to kill him if he doesn't hand over all his gold and money.

"At the very moment they were holding the knife against his throat, he saw me and begged me to warn you of his plight. He said to tell you to give me his whole fortune without fail, otherwise they will kill him. Look – I have his seven-league boots, which proves all I say."

Without hesitating for a second the woman gave Thumbkin everything. Apart from his habit of eating little children, she loved the ogre who was a very good husband to her.

Loaded with all the ogre's treasure, Thumbkin returned to his father's house where he was welcomed with great joy, and the family never went hungry again.

And what happened to the ogre and his wife? Well, Thumbkin never saw either of them again, which is probably just as well!

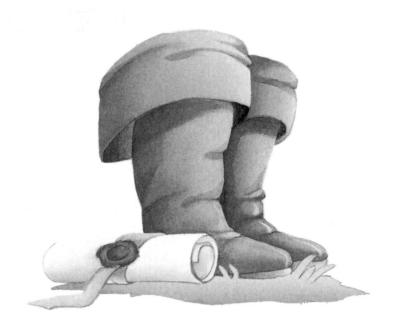